WOLF OF THORNS

THE SHIFTER REJECTED SERIES
BOOK FOUR

AMELIA SHAW

CHAPTER 1
TALIA

"Look me in the eyes." Galen clamped his hand on the young man's shoulder to reassure him that the pack would survive; that justice would be served for the loss of the wolf's parents. "You're family and we take care of our family, right Josh?"

The boy, who looked to be about fourteen, muttered his agreement. He didn't seem to share Galen's confidence, but his head full of dusty-blond curls bobbed when he nodded affirmation.

"Talia." Galen called my name and waved me over.

"Coming." I pushed the dark sunglasses up the bridge of my nose, making certain that my eyes were hidden from view behind the dark tinted lenses.

My eyes hadn't changed to red outside of a shift, but I wasn't taking any chances. I averted my gaze from Galen's, avoiding eye contact whenever possible. Which was harder to do than I thought.

Sunglasses had quickly become my favorite accessory.

I had faked more migraines in the short time since my eyes had first turned than I ever had in my life. It wasn't normal for a shifter to have long term ailments and Galen grew more concerned each day.

It was unfair to make him worry, considering the mysterious illness that plagued his father, but I didn't know what else to do.

Tell him the truth? The thought crossed my mind on more than one occasion, and I knew I risked losing his trust if I continued to withhold information and lie about my condition, but it was a risk I was willing to take.

At least until I had time to figure things out.

Galen would no doubt assume the red hue in my eyes was a side effect of the demon mark, and I would be inclined to agree. Except for the nagging suspicion—a gut feeling I'd had since I first saw my reflection at the lake—that it was something more.

Something far worse.

THE FACT that I believed something could be worse than a demon mark said a lot about the current state of my life.

I should have been happy. Galen had taken me in, saved me from a doomed fate as an outcast and rejected mate. He offered me a place among his pack and a new start on life. But with an all-out war with my former pack on the horizon, Galen's father continuing to decline in health with no answers in sight, and the increase in demon attacks... happiness felt like a pipe dream.

My weird red wolf eyes were the last thing Galen needed to worry about. I'd brought enough trouble with me as it was. He didn't need any more and neither did his pack.

"Earth to Talia." Galen waved a hand in front of my face and chuckled, but the worry lines pinching the corners of his eyes belied his casual tone. "Are you getting another migraine?"

"I thought I felt one coming on." I fidgeted with the oversized frames and made a mental note to order a new pair online—a pair that fit. "I'm hoping the sunglasses might stop it before it starts."

"Are you sure you're feeling okay?" Galen reached for me, his hand trailing down my arm to encircle my wrist.

I willed my pulse and breathing to stay within normal range and lied right to his face.

"Yeah, I'm good," I reassured him. "You'll be the first to know otherwise." I plastered a smile on my face. "Now, what can I help you with?"

"You remember Pam, right? Can you take Josh down to her house? She's got a spare bed and offered to take him in." Galen slid his hand into mine and laced our fingers together, giving a little squeeze before letting go. "Come find me when you're done."

He turned to Josh and extended his hand.

"Firm grip, kid. Remember what I said. I keep my word. Pam's a nice lady, so try not to give her a hard time, okay?"

JOSH PULLED BACK his hand with a nod, turned his back on his acting Alpha and walked off in the general direction of Pam's house without being formally dismissed.

A show of disrespect like that to the Alpha or one of his Betas would not have gone unnoticed or unpunished in my old pack, but Galen let the kid off without as much as a warning growl. I'd been raised to take a lack of response as a sign of weakness, but in the weeks I'd been with Galen, he'd opened my eyes and heart to the way a pack was meant to be run.

The way an Alpha was meant to lead.

Galen didn't rule his pack with fear and an iron fist. It wasn't about power and control for him—he was strong enough that he didn't need to prove that to anyone. He wanted what was best for the pack, for his people, and he took them into consideration with each and every decision he made or action he took.

Just like he did with Josh.

Galen knew that kid was broken-hearted and struggling after

the loss of his family during the Northwood pack's last attack on us. He was withdrawn, not actively disrespectful. Galen was compassionate enough to understand that. The Long Claw pack was lucky to have him as heir to the throne.

The same could not be said for my old pack.

Maddox wasn't Alpha material any more than I was his mate. Fated or not. The only person he was loyal to was his father. I'd learned that the hard way. If a wolf could give Destiny the middle finger and cast aside his fated mate just because Daddy told him to, then he could do it to anyone. And he wasn't a leader. He was a follower. None of the pack members would be safe under his rule.

The Northwood pack wasn't a pack at all.

Galen's wolves weren't the only ones lucky to have him. I was, too. Since he'd offered protection and taken me in, I'd seen first-hand what a functional pack looked like. But that wasn't the only thing I'd learned from Galen. If Maddox was the mate that Destiny had chosen for me, Galen was the mate I would have chosen for myself.

He listened when I spoke and took my feelings into consideration before he made a decision—even when it went against his protective Alpha nature. The feelings I had for Galen weren't based on a magical bond or some invisible connection that said two wolves had to be together because Fate decreed it.

My feelings for Galen were real, growing stronger by the day— and the timing couldn't have been worse.

I followed Josh to the house where Pam and her family would be fostering him until he was old enough to strike out on his own. He kept a brisk pace and his distance as we cut across the pack property. Josh wasn't much of a talker. I had no way of knowing for sure if he'd been that way before his family had been killed, but I recognized the distant, hollow look in his eyes and the slack expression on his face.

I'd seen it reflected back at me in the bathroom mirror the morning after my father had been murdered.

He wanted silence and I was happy to give it to him. As much as I would have appreciated any sign of kindness or expression of sympathy from my pack after my dad died, there were no words that could bring him back.

If there were, I probably would have tracked down a witch willing to recite those words, and bring back not only my dad, but my mom, too.

I was happy to leave Josh to his thoughts because it gave me a few moments of peace to focus on my own situation. But the round trip from dropping off Josh at Pam's wasn't nearly enough time to formulate a plan that would solve all my problems.

Truth was, they piled up so fast, I'd be lucky if I solved one.

The demon mark showed itself first. Galen knew about that one and we'd been working on figuring out how to get rid of it. That was progressing more slowly than I'd hoped, but the curses that plagued the local witch community and the demon attacks took precedence over my mark. We needed the witches' help, and they couldn't help if they were cursed.

Then the demons began attacking the town and the humans who lived there. If witches were susceptible to the Hell spawn running loose, the humans didn't stand a chance—so the pack offered its protection. Add in the Northwood attacks and the losses suffered in defense of Long Claw pack territory, and Galen's pack was spread thin.

My demon mark had been put on the back burner.

Of course, that was before my eyes turned red when I shifted. If Galen knew about that, he'd most likely drop everything else and divert all his attention and energy to solving my problem. Which is why I had to try and figure this out on my own.

The pack needed Galen. They needed him to focus on the

challenges he faced from all sides. I didn't want to be a distraction for him—or a weakness.

And I couldn't bear to be rejected. Again.

My heart wouldn't survive it a second time. I'd found a place where I belonged, and I would do whatever it took to stay here. Even if it meant withholding information from Galen.

"You don't have to keep following me." Josh slowed his pace to a crawl and craned his head over his shoulder. "Galen doesn't have to worry about me. I know where I'm going."

I bit back a yelp, startled out of my thoughts and the solace of quiet company.

"Sorry, didn't mean to scare you." Josh leaned against the trunk of an old sugar maple tree, arms crossed over his chest and one foot pressed against the base of the tree. "It's just, I don't need a... babysitter."

"Or a foster family?" I asked, calling him out on what I assumed he'd wanted to say but hadn't. He was quick to avert his eyes. That was confirmation enough that I was right. "You didn't scare me. I was just lost in my own thoughts. Do you know why Galen asked me to take you to Pam's?"

He shook his head, but refused to meet my gaze, giving the mushrooms clustered in the crook of an exposed tree root more attention than me.

"Well, since you're so interested, I'll tell you." I wasn't sure if he would find comfort in our shared tragedies, but I offered it anyway. "We're part of the same club, me and you. It's not all that exclusive, has zero perks, and pretty much near all of us would like to revoke our membership."

Josh's brows pinched together, deepening the creases that made a home on a face that should have been worry free.

"Yeah? So, you lost someone too. Everyone has." Denim scraped against the bark of the tree as he shifted his position and turned his back to me. "But my parents are dead. Both of them."

"So are mine. I lost my mom when I was young. My dad..." I choked back the sob that threatened to break free.

So much had happened in such a short time I hadn't properly grieved his loss. Of course, to do that I would have had to have a proper grave for my father, but the Northwood Alpha had taken that from me too.

"I lost my dad recently." I cleared my throat and started again. "He was murdered."

Josh rolled against the tree, turning to face me, and met my gaze. The flicker of anger I'd seen in his eyes blazed with an intensity that would have had me backpedaling if I hadn't recognized that emotion as well.

"By the same wolves who killed my parents." His voice had an edge like sharpened steel, and it cut just as deep. "You used to be one of them. My parents are dead because of you. Bet yours are too."

His words hurt. Just like they were meant to. Politics and power were the real motivators of the war Maddox and his father had started. Killing me was a bonus. I hadn't been the reason for the first attack on the Long Claw pack, but I made an easy target for the second one. Deep down, I knew that to be true. Like I knew I wasn't responsible for my father's death.

But it didn't make it hurt any less and it didn't make the thoughts I had—that Josh had just given voice to—go away.

"No." Somehow, I kept my voice even. "My dad was murdered for the same thing people have been dying over for centuries. Greed." I wrapped my arms around my middle and squeezed, as if I could hold back the sadness and anger over my father's death. The emotions constantly threatened to spill out of me. "Just like your family."

"Yeah," Josh mumbled, pushing himself off the tree trunk and starting to walk again. He cast a backward glance. "I'm sorry about your dad."

"I'm sorry about your parents too, Josh."

I dropped him off at Pam's, who was waiting on her porch with a comforting smile and a brood of kids varying in age peering out from the doorway behind her. Once Josh was inside, I went in search of Galen.

The sun hung low in the sky, taking its warm rays and higher temperatures with its descent below the horizon. Hues of orange and purple softened the transition from day to night but did little to ease the trepidation I felt over the appearance of the full moon.

I passed a few couples on my way back who had been tasked with splitting wood for the traditional post-run bonfire. The Long Claw pack celebrated the full moon each month with a hunt and, weather permitting, an outdoor after party. I'd been looking forward to it ever since Galen mentioned it.

Of course, that was before my wolf's eyes turned red whenever I shifted.

Galen must have finished pack business earlier than expected as he wasn't at the meeting house or with any of his Betas. Which left only one place to check—his father's house.

He sat on Max's porch steps, hands steepled in front of his face and seemingly lost in his thoughts. I'd crossed the street and made it halfway down the sidewalk before he finally heard my approach and rose to greet me.

"Talia, hey." Galen's smile lacked its usual luster and never reached his eyes. His brows pinched together, and his shoulders were slumped.

I could tell he was buried under the weight of worry over his father's declining health.

"Rough day?" I climbed the stairs and pulled him in for a hug that I needed as much as he did. "We're going to figure out what's wrong with him and get him the treatment he needs."

"I hope so." He pulled me close and tucked my head under his chin. "You ready for tonight?"

"I, umm..." I had practiced my excuse at least a hundred times during my walk back, but nerves got the better of me anyway. "I think I'll stay and keep an eye on Max."

"He wouldn't want you to miss out on the hunt, Talia." Galen pressed my body against his and massaged my lower back. "That will just make him feel worse than he already does."

"I've had a headache that's been trying to turn into a full-blown migraine all day. Trust me, I'm happy to stay home with him." I gave him one last squeeze before slipping out of his embrace and climbing the last step up onto the porch.

"I think you should see the pack doctor or maybe one of the witches." Galen grabbed my hand and stopped me from going inside. "Migraines like this aren't normal for us."

"It's just stress. You don't need to worry about me. I'm fine."

I hated that the lies came easier and that I'd gotten better at telling them. I needed to find out what was wrong with my eyes before Galen discovered the truth, or my new future would be over before it began.

CHAPTER 2

GALEN

The full moon offered a much-needed night of celebration for the pack. Between the demon attacks, the witches' curse, my father's illness, and the lives lost defending our property from the Northwood pack, there had been little to celebrate.

But the last thing I wanted to do right now was party.

Talia had been acting strangely. I would have liked to believe I was the cause for her erratic pulse and clammy hands whenever we were alone together, but I sensed that her odd behavior had little to do with the sparks between us or her migraines.

She'd been keeping something from me, and I needed to know her secret before things escalated out of control—I couldn't have her putting herself or the pack in more danger.

I followed her inside, down the hall and into my father's bedroom. His eyes lit up and color flushed his cheeks when she sat on the edge of his bed and pushed her sunglasses to the top of her head. My father enjoyed Talia's company, and the way she doted over him.

"What are you doing hanging out with an old man like me?

You should be with the others, getting ready for the hunt." My dad rested his hand over Talia's and gave a light squeeze. "I think I can manage one night on my own."

"Talia's not feeling well herself, Dad." I crossed the room and stood at his bedside. "I'll be out of contact during the hunt. What if something happens while I'm gone? Maybe I should stay here with the two of you."

"It's just a headache, Galen. Nothing that a little hydration and rest won't cure." Talia leaned in, gave my father a peck on the cheek and excused herself to the kitchen for a glass of water.

"She's sick? What's wrong? Why are you so worried?" My father hit me with a barrage of questions.

NONE of which I knew the answer to.

"She's been getting headaches. Migraines, actually, and lots of them, but swears she's fine." I grumbled the last bit and crossed my arms over my chest.

"But you don't believe her?" He wedged his elbows under him and tried to sit up, but adjusting his position cost him and caused a coughing fit. He waved off my attempts to help. When he caught his breath and could speak again, he asked me why my trust in Talia wavered.

"I don't know. I can't explain it." I raked my hands through my hair and paced the Persian rug covering the hardwood floor. "I do trust her, with the pack, with you, but..."

"Not with herself." There was a reason my father was the true Alpha. Even as sick as he was, his intuition was impeccable.

"Yeah." I let out an exasperated sigh, stopped pacing and turned to face him. I hoped he had the answers I needed—because I wasn't even sure what the problem was.

"Do you think it's possible that the reason you're having trust issues with Talia is because you don't trust yourself? That you're afraid of getting hurt. Or worse, hurting her?"

My father's keen intuition wasn't as admirable when it was directed at me.

I shook my head and pinched the bridge of my nose. "Just let me know if she says or does anything... off."

"Isn't she supposed to be babysitting me?" My father's laughter turned into another fit of coughing, worse than the last. He reached for his oxygen mask, smacking my hand away when I moved to help him put it on.

His words were muffled behind the bluish-tinged plastic mask, but I knew when I was being dismissed.

"How about I swing by later?" I paused in the doorway, one hand on the knob and the other on the door jamb. "I'll bring you a plate from the cookout."

He pulled the mask down, revealing the wide grin curving his mouth. "If there isn't a heaped helping of Carrie's banana cream pie on that plate, don't bother showing your face."

I PROMISED to bring the pie, then left him to rest after he finished his breathing treatment. I joined Talia in the kitchen.

"That cough sounds worse." She set her empty glass in the sink and braced her hip against the counter. "Maybe the doctor should increase his medicine or Sarah could prepare another poultice?"

"She's already prescribed the maximum dose and the witches haven't been able to come up with anything new." The smell of fresh coffee had me reaching for a mug from the cabinet above the coffee machine. "Shouldn't you be sticking to water?"

"Caffeine is good for headaches." She grabbed a mug for herself and poured us both a cup before the pot finished brewing. "I'll switch back to water after one or two cups."

"Are you sure you're going to be all right?" I grabbed the blue ceramic mug filled with black coffee and leaned back against the counter, taking a long pull of the steaming hot liquid.

"That's a loaded question, considering the demon mark on my wrist, don't you think?" Her eyes held a mischievous glint as she eyed me over the rim of her matching blue mug. She took a small sip of her coffee and set it down on the counter, looking down at it. "I just need to get some rest, Galen. I'll be fine. Promise."

She made a crisscross symbol over her heart to seal the promise, but I remained unconvinced.

"Okay, if you're sure?" I hated the nagging suspicion and growing divide I felt with her—especially when I couldn't pinpoint why.

It seemed like she wanted to distance herself from me. We spent less time together alone. Our conversations were shorter, more forced than usual. And I'd noticed she didn't meet my eyes the way she had before.

"I'm sure." She turned and rinsed out her mug, refilled it with water and clutched it in both hands. "I'm exhausted, Galen. I'm going to slip out of these jeans and into a pair of jammies, and you're going to go on the hunt and spend time with your pack."

She reached up and brushed a chaste kiss on my cheek, wished me good night and walked out of the kitchen.

I RECOGNIZED the confusion in Talia's eyes whenever we were alone together because I'd felt the same way when I first met her. How could my wolf feel an instant connection and driving need to protect her when she'd been another wolf's fated mate? It hadn't made sense then and four weeks with her had done little to clarify things in that regard, but there was no denying the feelings we shared.

And yet, that's exactly what she seemed to be doing. Denial. Big time.

Talia was pushing me away and I had no idea why. For the life of me I couldn't think of a single thing that I'd done to cause her to pull back. Was she still in love with her ex-fiancé, after everything he and that pack had done to her?

After everything I'd done for her.

My motives for bringing Talia home were selfish. I hadn't given much thought to what would happen to her beyond hostage negotiations with the Northwood pack. When I caught her near the Long Claw property lines, I hadn't planned on being the hero.

I hadn't planned on developing feelings for her.

Still, when I learned the truth about what her pack had done to her, I welcomed her into the pack with open arms. My heart had remained under lock and key for a while, but she broke in like a master thief and stole it anyway.

Maybe my father was right. My brain and my heart hadn't been on the same page since I saw Talia walking around town the day she'd planned to leave. Maybe I had been overreacting and there was nothing going on with Talia at all, beyond a simple migraine cluster.

Or maybe that nothing was really something. And not simple at all.

Whatever was going on with Talia, I needed to figure it out fast. If she was in more trouble, I had a right to know. She wasn't the only obligation I had. With my father lying immobile in that bed, the pack was my responsibility, and I was duty bound to protect each and every one of the pack members.

Not just the one I was falling in love with.

I LEFT through the back door, shed my clothes, shifted and slipped into the shadows of a row of Leyland cypress trees that ran along the inside of the fenced backyard.

And then I waited.

It was a full moon and whether she wanted to spend it with me, and my pack was debatable. What wasn't up for debate for any wolf, was the call of the moon itself. We had to answer it. The beautiful wolf who'd captured my attention was no exception.

The light breeze shifted direction and kept me downwind from the back door. I'd hoped to be less detectable by Talia's wolf. Women in the Northwood pack may have been forbidden from participating in playing offense and attacking other packs in the surrounding area, but they still learned to hunt—and use their sense of smell.

Besides, Talia may have been a little naive, but she wasn't an idiot.

I rolled in the dirt, dusting my coat for an added layer of camouflage and crawled further back into the tree line before waiting some more. I had decided to call it quits and give up on my stakeout when she came out the back door, bounded down the steps into the yard and shifted with an ease unseen in a wolf below the station of Beta.

She dug her claws into the lush grass and stretched back on her hind legs, before sprinting away.

When I saw her come out of the house, I hoped she'd had a change of heart, that she wanted to commune with me and the rest of the pack, for our wolves to hunt together.

The direction she headed said otherwise.

Talia wasn't running toward the bonfire or the pack, she was running away from them—away from me. What the hell had changed?

I planned to find out just as soon as the hunt was over. Once I was sure that Talia wasn't coming back and it was safe to step out of the shadows, I got dressed and joined Markus and Theo at the bonfire where the pack waited for me to kick off the festivities.

"Tonight, we complete another cycle and prepare to usher in a new moon and a new phase." I gazed out at the group gathered around the roaring fire.

THERE WERE LESS faces in the crowd staring back at me than there had been during the last full moon, and I felt every loss through the pack bond. The Long Claw pack members needed to run, to recharge under the beams of a full moon, and mend their broken hearts and battered souls.

But my heart wasn't in it.

It had been a long time since I'd felt this way. Since Jessie died.

Memories, dark and dangerous, crept into my mind. Remembering her and my past failures did little to improve my mood. Running through the woods with my packmates wasn't the distraction I needed. Still, I couldn't just run away like Talia had.

No matter how much I wanted to.

"I can see you all need this as much as I do. So, I'll just get right to it. Let the hunt begin," I called out, feeling the lie in my heart.

Tracking small game wasn't what I needed—or wanted. Not when there was larger prey to chase. My wolf itched to race after Talia as much as my human side did, but the pack needed me, and my wolf. We had to meet our obligations instead of giving in to paranoia and taking off on a whim.

Besides, I knew there would be plenty of time to question Talia after the run.

I cleared my mind and forced myself to be in the moment, hunting with my pack. My family. They needed me there with them. I owed them that and so much more. My participation in the hunt was the least that I could do for the people who fought and bled alongside me to protect our pack and property—our very way of life.

We had defeated the Northwood pack, sent them running

home with their tails tucked between their legs. But their Alpha was a power-hungry bastard, and he wouldn't stop until he got what he wanted. They'd be back, for sure.

The full moon festival was likely to be the last pack hunt for a long time. But I planned to do everything in my power to make sure 'a long time' didn't turn into 'forever'.

The smell of redwood cedar and moss-covered forest floor pulled me from the dark corners of my mind and back into the hunt. A young rabbit dashed out in front of me and then back into the thicket of thorn-ridden scrub brush when it caught sight of a wolf.

The cool, damp soil provided the perfect ground conditions for a silent approach. My paws sank into the dirt and left a trail of perfect impressions in my wake. The rabbit knew I was there. She could smell me as easily as I could her fear. But she'd lost sight of me from her hiding spot in the thicket and she couldn't hear my steps. I was the apex predator, and she was the prey.

It was the natural order of things.

I lunged, my front paws hit the ground with a thwump, just at the edge of the thorn bushes and flushed the rabbit out. But she didn't give up. She took off at full speed. The chase was on. I followed her, weaving around the trees, hurdling others that came running, before falling back and letting her go.

The rabbit lived to see another day.

Catch and release hadn't always been my preferred method of hunting wild game. After all, a wolf had to eat. But the world and the woods had gotten smaller over the years from deforestation and development. Less woodland meant less wildlife.

My father became something of a conservationist in my late teens and instituted a new policy. The animals who lived in the woods on our property were as much a part of the pack as any wolf. We protected the wildlife in order to protect our way of life.

"Eat the last rabbit today. Your belly is full, and your wolf is satiated. But what will you hunt tomorrow?"

My father's words echoed in my mind. He was right. With shrinking territories and less land to hunt, the predators outnumbered the prey. Years later the woods were a fertile hunting ground again. The animals were thriving.

Just like the pack under his rule.

He expected me to take his place. So did the pack. But I had big shoes to fill, and I wasn't sure my father's shoes would fit me.

We faced more challenges than we ever had. The Northwood pack seemed the least of our problems and that spoke volumes about the severity of the demon situation. Attacks on the local community had been increasing. What if I couldn't protect everyone who needed protection?

It wouldn't have been the first time I failed to keep someone safe.

I still had a few demons of my own—they lived inside my head. I sure as hell didn't need actual demons running loose around the town, possessing and killing locals.

One problem at a time. The first thing I needed to deal with was whatever Talia was hiding from me. She'd been looking forward to the hunt for weeks and bailed at the last minute. That wasn't like her.

Neither was keeping secrets.

It was high time I figured out her secrets. I hightailed it out of the woods, shifting back before I reached the tree line. I retrieved the pile of clothes I had stashed by an old ash tree and dressed before I headed back to the bonfire.

A few of the pack members had returned from hunting early and manned the tables covered with potluck dishes. I grabbed a couple of paper plates and loaded them up with a little of everything from main dishes to sides. A third plate had been reserved for a huge helping of the banana cream pie my father had requested.

After a quick text to my Betas to let them know that I was calling it an early night and taking food home for the Alpha, I thanked the volunteers serving up helpings of home-cooked food and said my goodbyes.

The neighborhood was quiet and dark with everyone down at the bonfire celebrating. My father's house was no exception. The outside security lights failed to trip when I passed the motion sensor, and the only light came from the front bedroom where my father spent his days and nights.

I balanced the plates overloaded with food and went inside in search of Talia, who was curled up asleep on the loveseat in the family room. She looked so peaceful I hated to disturb her, but we were overdue for a conversation. Thankfully, a double portion of banana cream pie would hold my father's attention long enough for Talia and I to have a semblance of privacy.

"Talia." With a feather-light grip on her shoulders, I shook her awake. "Wake up, we need to talk."

"What?" She propped her head up on one hand and rubbed the sleep from her eyes with the other. "Galen, what's going on?"

"Hey, that's my line." I brushed a strand of her golden-red hair from her face and tucked it behind her ear. "You need to tell me what's wrong, Talia."

THE SOFT HONEYSUCKLE notes of her perfume were enough to draw me in and bring me to my knees. I hadn't been this close to her in days, except for the brief hug on the porch earlier, and I missed her. The comfort of her touch and embrace. Just being with her was enough to cool my temper and steady my mind.

Part of me wanted to curl up on the couch beside her and

forget about confronting her. Whatever was bothering her could wait until morning.

Except it couldn't.

If I put off talking to Talia for another day, another problem would pop up. I had too many fires to deal with as it was. I needed to extinguish this one before it burned out of control.

"Nothing's wrong." She pushed herself to a sitting position and crossed her arms over her chest. "Why do you keep asking me that?"

"Because your body language and the wall you're putting up between us says otherwise." I plopped down on the empty couch cushion beside her and draped my arm around her shoulders. "You can tell me. Whatever it is. Just talk to me, please."

"Galen, there's nothing wrong besides a few headaches." She reached up and clasped her hand on mine and gave a gentle squeeze. "I'm just tired."

"Too tired to go for a run, right?" I reined in the flare of anger over her outright lie.

She wasn't just tired, and it wasn't just headaches. I gave her an opportunity and she lied straight to my face.

Talia averted her gaze, focusing on her hands in her lap as she picked at a loose string on the hem of her shirt.

She knew that she'd been busted.

"I was." Talia inched over to the side, putting a little distance between us. "But my wolf was restless. I guess the call of the full moon was too much for her and I knew the bonfire was too much for me. We compromised and went for a run around the neighborhood."

To her credit, she had the conviction to stick with her story. Which left me in a tough spot. Did I call her out or let it lie?

I knew I couldn't leave it alone. I had to say something, get it off my chest before the problem festered and ate away at me.

"Fine. You changed your mind and needed to go for a run after all." I gave her one small victory.

I supposed there was a slim chance that was the real reason, but she was still hiding something from me. So, I pressed her on it.

"I want you to know... No, I need you to know that I know there is something going on with you. That you're keeping something from me. I don't know what it is, or why you won't tell me, but you should also know as acting Alpha of the Long Claw pack I have both the power and the authority to make you tell me."

Talia's eyes widened and her lips parted as she scooted further away on the couch. It pained me to see even a glimmer of fear in her eyes and to know that my words put it there, but I couldn't afford to take any more risks.

I needed to know that I could trust her as much as I wanted to, because if I couldn't, we were both headed for heartbreak.

I leaned in and when she didn't pull away, pressed my lips against her forehead in a chaste kiss. I hoped I wasn't about to overplay my hand, but she'd backed me into a corner and left me with no choice.

"I care about you, Talia. More than you know. More than I wanted to admit to myself until this very moment, but I can't have secrets between us. You're going to have to tell me one way or another."

CHAPTER 3

TALIA

The silence in the house after Galen left was deafening. Even Max kept to himself. He hadn't called for me once since the front door clicked shut behind his son. No game of cards or gossip before bed.

Unless there was a sedative in that banana cream pie, Max had heard his son's ultimatum. It seemed he was giving me space, rather than advice on what I should do.

Telling Galen the truth was the obvious answer. It solved many problems. But it created so many others.

I wouldn't tell him. Not unless I had to. Or Galen forced me to. As acting Alpha, he could. The question was whether or not he would.

Galen was many things, but cruel wasn't one of them. I didn't believe he would use his position to get me to talk unless I forced him into it. It seemed we were at an impasse.

But I was the one running out of time.

I couldn't hold Galen off forever. I needed to figure out what was causing my eyes to turn red when I shifted—and fast. Otherwise, I would leave Galen no choice but to pull the pack bonds and make me tell him.

Magic was my last shot at figuring out what was wrong with me. If anyone could figure it out, it would be Sarah. I grabbed my phone off the coffee table and sent her a text inviting her to lunch the next day.

There was a little cafe in town. The menu was simple, but everything was made fresh daily, and the people were nice. I used to wait tables there part time. Of course, that was before Maddox and his father tossed me out and ran me off.

I hadn't been back since I gave my notice with the intention of leaving town, and worried my reappearance would raise a lot of unwanted questions. But I needed a place on neutral ground. Not between two rival packs. Between the Long Claw pack and the coven.

And neutral ground for me.

Town was considered a safe zone. It was as much my place as any and had nothing to do with any man in my life. Past or present.

Sarah texted me back with a yes in all caps, followed by several exclamation points. From the look of her text, I wasn't the only one who was feeling the need to cross the Long Claw property line.

Gratitude didn't begin to describe the way I felt toward Galen and the pack for everything they've done for me. They hadn't just taken me in like a rogue or a stray. They fought with and for me.

But whatever caused the change in my eyes wasn't something that could be fixed with pack bonds. I needed to talk to a witch. I needed Sarah's help and that was a conversation better had away from the pack and the coven.

The less people that knew about my problem the better. At least until I knew what my problem actually was.

Relieved that Sarah had agreed to meet me, I curled back up on the couch and let sleep claim me.

The demon who had marked my wrist plagued my dreams. Even when I closed my eyes, I couldn't escape him. I tossed and turned for hours in snatches of restless sleep before I finally gave up just before sunrise.

I shuffled into the kitchen, put on a fresh pot of coffee and texted Galen my plans for the day. His response didn't arrive until I was well into my second cup of coffee and consisted of two clipped sentences.

Have fun. I'll send someone to escort you.

"Damn it." I slapped my palms on the counter, bowed my head and let out a deep breath. "Someone to escort me?"

I'd forgotten about Galen's new rule. Which admittedly had more to do with the demon attacks than it did with the problems with me and the Northwood pack.

I hadn't really left pack lands since Galen and I went to a neighboring town to see a coven of dark witches for a cure to the curse. There hadn't been a need to go anywhere else since then. I loved spending time with Galen and helping out with the pack whenever I could.

I still did.

But I couldn't shift around any of them, given my eyes. That meant no more shifts on patrol, no more volunteer hours with the children's center where young wolves learned how to use and control the gifts we'd been given.

Pretty much all volunteer work was off limits.

Which put my status in the pack on shaky ground. Wolves were expected to pull their weight, contribute to the community. I couldn't do that in my condition, and I couldn't tell anyone why.

I didn't want to land myself in hot water with the Long Claw pack. I had enough trouble as it was. I had to find a way to talk with Sarah about my problems without our escort overhearing and reporting back to Galen.

"Damn, damn. Double damn." I cursed more in the minutes after reading Galen's text than I had in a long time.

"Talia, are you talking to me?" Max coughed a few times and cleared his throat. "Is everything okay down there?"

"Shit." I muttered under my breath. For a moment I'd forgotten I wasn't alone.

"I heard that too." Max chuckled. "The body's going, but my ears are still working fine."

"Good to know." I couldn't help but laugh. Max seemed to be in a good mood, and it was contagious. "You hungry? Or are you still full of all that banana cream pie you ate last night?"

"How about a cup of coffee with a little conversation on the side." Max's voice carried down the stairs from his second-floor bedroom and I could hear the smile in his tone as he called out his order.

"Coming right up." I hoped he couldn't sense the grimace on my face when I replied.

He'd heard me mumble under my breath. There was no way he hadn't heard my conversation with Galen the night before. Of course, he wanted to talk about it, and no doubt offer some sage fatherly advice.

It made me sad to think Max's advice would probably be better than any advice my own father would have given. He'd never been much of a talker or a problem solver, but I sure loved the hell out of him and missed him every day.

Staying with Max took the edge off the pain of loss, but when everything hit the fan, it was my father whose shoulder I'd wanted to cry on.

I sliced a cinnamon raisin bagel in two, plopped both halves in the toaster, and poured Max's coffee while I waited for the bread to brown. According to the dial on the toaster, I had two and a half minutes to come up with an honest answer that would appease the old Alpha's curiosity without actually telling him the truth.

The problem was, I couldn't think of anything.

With his breakfast, and a refill for me, on the serving tray, I headed upstairs and prepared to expand my web of lies.

"Is that cinnamon raisin I smell?" Max tapped the mattress, inviting me to sit on the bed with him.

He reached out and unfolded the legs hidden underneath the tray so I could set it down over his lap.

"Coffee can upset an empty stomach. So, I made you a bagel." I offered a warm smile as I took a seat on the corner of the bed. "How'd you sleep?"

"Better than you did down on that lumpy sofa, I would say." Max pulled off a chunk of the toasted bagel and popped it in his mouth. "What's going on, Talia?"

"Well, the cure for the witches' curse still works. There hasn't been a single witch infected." I reached for my mug and took a long pull of the light and sweet coffee. "Of course, you already knew that. The demons are still attacking the town and I'm pretty sure the Northwood pack is planning another attack of their own. So, you know, just another day in the neighborhood."

Max studied me over the rim of his coffee cup, one eyebrow arched in question, as if he hoped I'd say more without being prodded.

"If I wanted a status report, I would have asked Galen. I'm asking about you." He set his coffee down and took another bite of his bagel before pushing the tray away.

"That's all you're going to eat?" I asked, concerned over his decreasing appetite.

"I'm still digesting all the pie I ate last night." He gave his stomach a little pat. "And you're deflecting."

"I am not." I punctuated the lie with a huff for effect, but the stern look on Max's face said he wasn't buying it. "I'm fine. Really. I wish everyone would stop worrying. There's nothing wrong.

"If anyone understands how frustrating it can be having people hover over you, asking if you're all right every minute of the day, it's me." His weary smile never reached his eyes. "But they worry because they care about you. Especially Galen."

Guilt hit me like a harpoon to the chest. If my heart were a target, Max would have hit dead center.

"I know. I care about him too." I lowered my gaze and picked at a loose thread on the quilt covering Max's bed. I couldn't lie and maintain eye contact. "If something was wrong, he'd be the first to know."

"I hope that's true, Talia." Max leaned back into the pillows propping himself up with a sigh. "I'd hate to see either of you hurt again."

Sparing Galen from any more pain was precisely what I'd been trying to do by not telling him about my eyes. The fact that I was terrified about what it meant to shift into a red-eyed wolf may have also had something to do with it.

"You're still tired. I'm sorry I woke you so early." I stood up, set my cup on the tray and picked it up on my way out. "Go back to sleep. I'm going to jump in the shower."

"You don't have to rush off. I'm not tired." Max's eyelids belied his words, dropping like a Broadway curtain closing before I cleared the threshold.

It was just as well. He didn't need to worry about me any more than Galen did.

I opted for a hot bath instead of a shower. A long soak was better for relieving the tension knots built up in my muscles from stress and a lack of exercise. The run last night had been far shorter than I'd have liked. I stayed in the tub until my fingers pruned and the water was turning cold.

The house was spotless by the time one of Galen's Betas

showed up to escort me to town. I'd been anxious and unable to sit still, so I'd channeled that nervous energy into cleaning every surface from top to bottom.

NOT A SINGLE COBWEB or dust bunny survived.

"Hey, Talia." A male voice called out over the sound of the vacuum.

I spun around, wielding the lightweight vacuum like a baseball bat.

"Whoa, easy there, slugger." Theo, one of Galen's Betas, stood inside the foyer with his hands raised in the air. "I knocked a few times and figured you couldn't hear me over the vacuum."

"You scared the hell out of me." I propped the vacuum against the back of the couch and clutched a hand over my still-racing heart.

"Sorry." Theo's easy-going smile went a long way to settling my nerves. "So, lunch and a little window shopping with Sarah? Sounds like a fun girls' day."

"It would be, except for the chaperone." I swapped out the vacuum cleaner for a lightweight beige cargo jacket that complimented my cream-colored tee shirt, jeans and brown suede ankle boots.

"Hey, I'm not happy about the babysitting detail either, but Alpha's orders." Theo opened the front door and motioned for me to lead the way. "Ladies first."

"I'll drive." I grabbed my keyring and purse from the cherry accent table in the foyer and made a beeline for my car.

"How about no." Theo shut the door behind him, jogged up beside me and dangled his key fob in front of me. "I always drive."

"Babysitter and chauffeur. I hope you're getting paid double." I waited for him to unlock the doors of his pickup truck and climbed into the passenger seat.

"Damn, I could have gotten paid for this gig?" Theo turned the engine and backed down the driveway. "How come nobody told me that?"

"Well, maybe you should take it up with the Alpha." I dug my phone out of my bag and texted Sarah to let her know we were on our way.

"Yeah, right." Theo chuckled and shifted into drive. "Buckle up."

He made casual conversation about the hunt the night before and the potluck afterward. My absence had not gone unnoticed, and the shifters loved to gossip as much as anybody. Apparently, I'd been the talk of the pack.

If well wishes solved problems, the members of the Long Claw pack would have fixed me right up.

"Pam whipped up one of her famous homebrew headache cures." Theo spared a glance in my direction before returning his attention back to the road. "Works like a charm too, on account of all the alcohol in it. She asked Galen to drop it off for her."

Theo had been doing most of the talking. I wasn't in the mood for small talk. Maybe it was my guilty conscience, but the whole thing felt more like a fishing expedition than an actual conversation.

Still, it was better if I talked than kept quiet and raised more suspicion about my wellbeing.

"I'll have to stop by her house and thank her. I wanted to check in on Josh anyway, to make sure he's settling in okay."

"I think he'd appreciate that. According to Pam, you made quite the impression on the kid."

Theo suddenly slammed on the brakes and threw the truck into reverse. "Oh, hell. You better get Sarah on the phone."

"What? What is it?" I gripped the dashboard and held on for dear life as Theo raced backward through the lunch rush traffic. Then I saw what he must have seen moments earlier. "Oh, oh no.

Theo, stop the truck. We can't leave. We have to help her. Theo, stop the truck."

There was a woman ahead, struggling to defend herself from a demon attack. She would be as good as dead if we didn't stop to help her.

Theo ignored my pleas, so I grabbed the steering wheel and jerked hard to the right. All four tires screamed in protest and a cloud of black smoke from burning rubber rolled out from under the truck. The pickup bucked, tilted up on two wheels and slammed back down, rocking the cab on impact before coming to a halt.

"Have you lost your damn mind?" Theo growled, his eyes ringed with gold. His wolf was close to the surface.

"She's going to die." I pressed the unlock button and reached for the door handle, but Theo relocked the doors before I could get it open.

"Yeah? Well, I'm going to die if I let you out of the truck and within a hundred feet of that thing." He righted the truck and prepared to hit the gas. "Because Galen would kill me if something happened to you."

"I'll tell him you didn't have a choice." I hit the unlock button with my left index finger and jerked the door handle with my right.

"Son of a bi—" Theo reached for me, but he was too slow.

I hopped out of the cab and rushed across the street to help the woman who was being brutally attacked.

"How are you supposed to tell Galen it's your fault if you're unconscious or dead?" Theo ran up beside me. "You are a stubborn woman, you know that?"

"Yeah, I guess I am." I shot him a lopsided grin.

I never thought being called stubborn was something I'd enjoy. It wasn't usually considered a compliment. But, after years of being a 'yes' woman, bending over backwards to please everyone and be the wolf or mate they wanted me to be, being called stubborn felt like a badge of honor.

Theo may have said stubborn, but it sounded an awful lot like independent to me.

"Just stay back by the truck, okay? You need to be able to get out of here if this doesn't go according to plan. Not that I actually have a plan." Theo shook his head, but I caught the feral grin on his face before he turned and charged at the demon.

I wanted to rush after him and help fend off the demon but hung back near the truck like he asked. It was the least I could do. After all, he was defying an order from his Alpha, ignoring his responsibility as my bodyguard for now, and battling a demon to save a perfect stranger.

Besides, I'd likely only hinder him in a fight. Theo would be more worried about keeping me safe and would end up getting injured—or worse, killed.

The best thing I could do for everyone was stay put.

Theo shifted mid-sprint and landed on all fours using his body to shield the woman. She was a witch; I could now tell from the magic she was throwing the demon's way. She was already bloodied, beaten, and her breathing ragged by the time Theo reached her, but somehow, she found the strength to manifest one more spell.

A burst of magic smacked the demon in the face, knocked it backward and provided the opening Theo needed. He snarled, lunged at the demon and sank his sharp teeth into the creature's neck, tearing out its throat.

The creature collapsed on the sidewalk. Thick, black blood ran over the curb and onto the street. It looked dead, but I knew from experience demons were harder to kill than that.

"We need to go." I cupped my hand beside my mouth to project my voice. "Like now."

Theo nudged the witch with his snout. She buried her fingers into the thick fur at the nape of his neck and leaned on the Long Claw Beta for support.

"I'll drive." I helped the witch into the passenger seat, while Theo hopped into the bed of the truck.

I hit the gas and never let off until we crossed over the pack's property line and were back within the protection of the coven's wards.

Saving the witch had been dangerous, but that was nothing compared to telling Galen what we'd done.

CHAPTER 4

GALEN

"You did what?" I roared. Anger and my rising blood pressure flushed my cheeks with heat. "She could have been killed."

I lunged at Theo, fisted my hands in his shirt, and yanked him out of the chair across from the beige couch in my father's living room.

"He only did what I asked." Talia stepped forward, her hand outstretched as if she would reach for me, but she hesitated and lowered her arm back down to her side. "The witch would have died."

"And that was worth the risk? Is her life more valuable than yours?" I released my Beta and raked my fingers through my hair, tugging at the ends. "Haven't I done enough to protect the witches? Hasn't the pack sacrificed enough?"

"Galen," Talia scolded, shock and disappointment over my words in her voice and eyes—though she'd yet to meet my gaze. "This isn't a one-sided relationship. The coven has helped you too. They put up the wards, they helped heal your injured pack members after the attack and any of them would stand beside you to replenish your ranks if you asked."

"I know." I growled, pacing the floor to take the edge off my temper. "It's just... If something happened to you, I'd never forgive myself."

"You would have done the same thing." She jutted her chin and held her ground.

She had me there. I would have done the same thing, and it was hard to stay mad at her for that.

But that didn't stop me from trying.

After all, there were mitigating circumstances. Disobeying an order from a Beta acting under my authority and taking unnecessary risks with her life weren't the only things Talia was guilty of. There was still the matter of the secret she was keeping from me.

I struggled to separate my personal feelings for Talia and pack business and held onto my anger a little longer than usual.

"Of course, I would have done the same thing, Talia, but I'm the acting Alpha. I get to make those decisions. My Betas make those decisions when I'm not around." I pinched the bridge of my nose and let out a deep breath. "I thought I could trust you to abide by those decisions."

"You can." Talia still refused to meet my gaze, but I saw tears spill over her lashes and track down her cheeks. "Galen, I..."

She hesitated and for a moment I thought she was going to finally open up to me; trust me enough to explain what was going on with her.

But she never did.

Talia stood there, staring at the floor as if the answers to her problems were hidden in the carpet fibers.

I wanted to take her into my arms, hold her close and keep her safe from the darkness that haunted her, but she refused to let me in.

No matter how many times I asked.

As if that weren't enough, she had put Theo's life in danger. Two wolves against one demon. The odds weren't in their favor, but she risked herself and my Beta anyway. For a random witch she didn't even know.

I couldn't trust her judgment, or her motivation and I hated that more than anything. If she would just talk to me, I wouldn't feel the need to question everything she said or did.

The distance Talia had created between us was growing and I had no idea how to make it stop.

"The witch, is she going to be okay?" I'd been so distracted by what could have happened that I hadn't even asked about the woman they rescued.

Talia was right. The coven was an important alliance. We needed their help as much as they needed ours. But even if we didn't, I would have still cared about what happened to the injured woman. I wasn't a heartless bastard.

Just a heartbroken one.

"Sarah said she'll make a full recovery. She'll stay with the healers for another day or two and then move to more permanent housing with the coven." Theo stood with his feet apart and hands clasped behind his back.

His body language was non-confrontational, but not submissive. Theo wouldn't have disobeyed an order had Talia not jumped out of the truck, but I knew my Beta well enough to know he didn't think they were wrong to save the witch.

Truth be told, I didn't, either.

That was the part of being an Alpha that I struggled with. If one wolf disobeyed and I did nothing, I would appear weak, and the pack could fall into chaos. Or worse, I could be challenged.

If I punished my friends, the people closest to me, I would be cursed to live a lonely life. Heavy is the head that wears the crown, indeed.

"Theo, I can't let this slide. If word got out about your disobedience..."

"He didn't disobey you. I did." Talia's defiant tone drew my attention back to her but once again her gaze was everywhere but on me.

"I suppose you're right." The thought of punishing Talia hurt my head and my heart.

A growl rumbled up the back of my throat. I practically wore a path in the carpet, pacing the room as I racked my brain for an alternative solution to an impossible situation.

"This is stupid." I bemoaned the circumstances. "Remind me why being Alpha is such a great gig again?"

"It's hard to argue in favor of something you have no interest in. Being Alpha is all you, buddy." Theo chuckled and raised his hands briefly before dropping them back to his sides. "You've got nothing to worry about from me."

"We're practically at war with the Northwood pack, not to mention a legion of demons, and I'm supposed to punish members of my pack for putting others before themselves? A sentiment I agree with?"

"I thought it was because Talia disobeyed you." Theo's tone was light, and I appreciated his sense of humor more than ever.

"Hey." Talia, on the other hand, did not. "Throwing me under the bus. Nice."

"What if there's no bus to throw you under?" I stopped pacing and rounded on both of them as a thought occurred to me. "I was so focused on what an Alpha is supposed to do in a situation like this that I forgot no one outside of this room knows that I gave an order to begin with."

"So..." Talia hesitated. "You're not going to do anything?"

"I'm not going to do anything because I don't have to do anything." The weight of acting as judge, jury and executioner slipped from my shoulders. I felt like I could breathe and think for the first time since they'd returned from town. "Tell me about the demons. How many were there? Anything new to report?"

"I saw half a dozen at most." Theo dropped down onto the far left cushion and draped his arm over the back of the couch. "Only one was after the witch. The rest I spotted seemed hell bent on destroying the few stores left in town. Other than that, there isn't much I can tell you. It was a bit of a blur after Talia jumped out the passenger door, to be honest."

Talia gave a side-eyed look at his comment about her vacating the cab of the truck. "I didn't notice anything different," she said. "In fact, it felt eerily similar to the night I was attacked."

"You think it was trying to mark the witch? The same way you were marked?"

Had it been anyone else besides one of my Betas been in the room, I wouldn't have mentioned Talia's mark.

So far, they, alongside a select few in the coven, were the only ones who knew about her condition. We hadn't even shared it with my father; having agreed the worry and stress would be too much for him.

He'd kill me if he ever found out. I intended to make sure he never did. Besides, it's not like there was anything he could do about the mark in his condition. He needed more rest. Not more stress.

"You think it was trying to mark her?" I prompted again. "Like they did with you?"

Talia and I had been so focused on her mark that I hadn't given much, if any, thought to someone else being marked. The witches hadn't said anything and to my knowledge, none of them bore a mark like Talia's.

"I don't know." She rubbed the scar on her wrist. "I mean, it's possible. Right?"

"Demons are running loose around town." Theo stretched his

legs out in front of him and crossed them at the ankles. "I'd say just about anything is possible at this point."

"It's not just locally." I'd taken a call for my father from the shifter council not long after Talia and Theo left and brought them up to speed on what I'd been told by the representative I spoke with. "It's happening all over the country. Demons are attacking witches and the packs that protect them."

"Seriously?" Theo uncrossed his legs and shot to his feet. "What is the council planning to do about it?"

"Exhaust all options." I shook my head and let out a frustrated sigh. "Whatever that means. After they discuss the options to death, no doubt. You know how the council is. All talk and very little action. They leave everything up to the local packs."

'Yeah, but this is different. You're talking about a full-blown, nationwide demon infestation. They have to do something." Theo gave voice to the same thoughts I'd had when I spoke to the council member.

I wished I could share his faith in the council. My experience with them as liaison for the Long Claw pack had taught me otherwise.

"Maybe. But I'm not holding my breath. We can't wait around for them to decide to act. We have to protect our pack and be ready for another demon attack on pack land." Easier said than done when I had no idea what the demons were up to.

I'd expressed as much to the council member, but they didn't seem concerned with the motives of the attacks as much as the losses incurred by them.

Even with all my years' experience as the son of an Alpha and as heir to the throne of our pack, I wondered if I would ever truly understand politics.

"And the town?" Talia sat in the recliner and clutched a decorative pillow crocheted with "wolves are man's best friend" across the front, to her chest. "People are getting hurt. Are we just going to retreat behind property lines and leave everyone else to the demons?"

"We can't protect everyone." Theo caught the throw pillow she tossed at him before it connected with his head. "Hey, I'm just being realistic. We literally cannot protect everyone. There aren't enough of us."

"I have people that matter to me in town. Friends and coworkers from the cafe." Talia wiped her eyes with the back of her hand. "They were good to me."

"Because they didn't know what you are." Theo shrugged under our pointed glares. "You think they'd be so hospitable if they knew you have fangs and claws?"

"Compared to the demons running around? Yeah, I think they would." Talia scoffed and crossed her arms over her chest.

"Touché." Theo nodded his agreement. "You've got me there."

"He's not wrong though, Talia." I hated being the bearer of bad news and disappointing her, but Theo was right. We couldn't save everyone. "It's a numbers game and the Northwood pack's power grab cost us loved ones we couldn't afford to lose, even without a demon uprising on top of that."

Tears spilled over her lashes and tracked down her cheeks, but she brushed them away with her fingers. Her pain was my pain. It didn't matter what was going on between me and Talia. The problem with the demons was bigger than all of us.

I swallowed my pride, crossed the room to close the distance between us and rested my hand on her shoulder. She reached up, rested her hand over mine and leaned into my touch; her tear-stained cheek pressed against my forearm.

"I know." Talia sniffled away the last of her tears and clung to my arm. "It just sucks."

"Talk about an understatement." Theo collapsed on his side and stretched out over the length of the couch. "At least we had the full moon festival. One last hoorah before all hell breaks loose."

"Thank you for that little bit of optimism." I gave Talia's shoulder a little squeeze and slipped my hand out from under hers, before pacing again.

Theo's jaded humor was the kick in the ass I needed. Maybe we could all do with a dose of optimism.

"We have to stop sitting around complaining about how horrible things are and feeling sorry for ourselves and do something." I was the acting Alpha, and I had to do something other than bitch and moan. "Theo, find Markus and David. We're going to need to rally the troops and increase the perimeter watch."

"On it." He pulled his cell from his front jeans pocket and texted my other Betas. "And you'll be?"

Theo left his question hanging. It wasn't a challenge to my authority. As one of my seconds, he needed to know where I would be and what I would be doing if there was an emergency and he needed to reach me. If he couldn't, he needed to know that he had authority to make decisions for the pack in my stead.

I trusted my Betas completely. If I hadn't, I wouldn't have promoted them to the position. Their judgment was as sound as mine. Sometimes more so when the three of them acted together.

"I'll take Talia and we'll talk to the coven. We need to make sure the wards remain secure." I gave myself a quick pat down to check for my phone, keys and wallet. "And see if there is a way they can do something for the town. If they can't ward the whole town, maybe they can protect the homes and stores of people who haven't evacuated."

I checked in on my father and brought him up to speed before Talia and I parted ways with Theo. My Betas had their mission and we had ours.

All we needed to do was convince the coven to help us. Easier said than done. They came to the pack for shelter. Not to enlist in a militia against the evil undead. Marguerite, the coven's high priestess, had asked for my help when the attacks began and offered her services warding the pack's property lines in return.

Marguerite bartered for everything. The coven's magic wasn't free, and she never asked or expected anything for free for herself or any other witch. She kept a level playing field for anyone who dealt with the coven, and I appreciated that.

Talia and I helped the coven when we went on a road trip in search of a cure for the demon curse. In exchange, Marguerite agreed to help Talia with her demon mark. We came back with a supposed cure, but the high priestess couldn't remove the mark.

The way I saw it, the coven still owed us a favor. I doubted Marguerite would agree. Magic came at a cost and the high priestess set a high price.

I just hoped it was a price we could afford.

CHAPTER 5

TALIA

Galen and I were on our way to meet with the coven. I had messaged Sarah as soon as we got back to pack lands, and she'd hurried back too and checked over the witch we'd saved. Then Theo had taken me to Galen's dad's house, and Galen had almost exploded with rage when he heard what had happened.

I was glad he'd calmed down so quickly. And now he wanted to talk with Marguerite about the demon attacks, I was pleased he wanted me there, too. I had an ulterior motive, of course. I needed to talk to Sarah about my demonic wolf eyes.

Easier said than done with Galen breathing down my neck.

He only wanted to protect me, to keep me safe. I knew that. Just like I knew how he felt about me. The attraction between us was undeniable and I could sense that he cared for me as much as I did him. Which is why I was so scared he'd find out something was wrong with me.

I hated putting distance between us and the growing resentment I felt for the lack of space and independence. Fear and insecurity had spread in my mind like an invasive weed ever since I'd been attacked by the demon.

I needed to figure out what the hell was wrong with me before I ruined everything.

I'd planned to talk with Sarah over lunch about the way my eyes changed colors when I shifted, but thanks to the demon, that never happened. The attack screwed everything up and I couldn't help but wonder if that was the point.

Were the demon mark and my red eyes connected? Were they able to track me through the brand on my skin? I had so many questions and so far, zero answers. I'd hoped Sarah could at least help figure out why my irises started turning red in my wolf form because I couldn't avoid looking Galen in the eye forever.

All I could do was find an opportunity to get Sarah alone and hope we came up with something. If not a permanent solution, at least a glamor spell or potion that hid my red eyes from Galen and the rest of the pack.

As far as plans went, mine was almost nonexistent.

Sarah rushed out to the truck to greet us when we pulled up to the witches' encampment. "Are you crazy, jumping in like that when a demon was involved?"

"I was wondering the same thing," Galen chuckled. "But it's not the first time she's tussled with one of those things. She's becoming a regular demon hunter." Galen switched off the ignition and hopped out of the driver's side of the old pickup.

"Brave and stupid." Sarah bumped the passenger door closed with her hip after I climbed out of the cab of the truck.

"Did you two give each other talking points?" I shook my head and draped my arm around the closest friend I had excluding Galen, and leaned in to whisper in her ear. "I need your help."

It was a risk with Galen so close. He could have heard my plea to Sarah. And if he had, he would no doubt have picked up on the inflection. Galen had come to know me better than anyone, even my ex. He would have known that I wasn't asking on behalf of the pack.

I needed to be careful. To play it cool and not give anything away. I couldn't afford to blow the one opportunity I might have to talk with Sarah before all hell broke loose.

Again.

"Great minds think alike, I guess." Sarah wrapped her arm around my lower back and matched my pace. "Why are we whispering? What's going on?"

"Girl talk." I answered with a white lie on the off-chance Galen wasn't as distracted by pack business as I thought.

"Ahh, relationship advice. Love potions aren't really my thing. Now, lust on the other hand, is my specialty." Sarah spoke in a teasing tone, her voice still a murmur.

She slipped out from under my arm and walked ahead, ushering us toward a small campfire where Marguerite toiled over a steaming cauldron.

"I'm going to borrow Talia for a minute. You two catch up. We won't be long." Sarah grabbed my hand and started to lead me back the way we'd come.

"Now? Your conversation can't wait?" Galen thrust his arm out like a barricade, stopping us in our tracks.

"Girl talk." Sarah stole my line and tossed it at Galen as if he wouldn't question that as well. When he arched a brow and opened his mouth to do just that, she elaborated. Much to my embarrassment. "You know, cramps and bloating, back pain. I'm just going to whip her up a quick elixir. We'll be back before you know it."

That wasn't what I'd meant by girl talk. The heat of embarrassment scorched my cheeks, no doubt turning them a flattering shade of beet red.

Galen's suddenly wide-eyed, slack-jawed expression said it all. He'd been caught off guard by Sarah's brash response and clearly had no intention of questioning it further. I had to give her credit. The witch was a genius.

Sarah created an opportunity and I needed to make the most of it.

"Okay, what in Hecate is going on?" Sarah dragged me away from the campfire in the direction of the truck.

"When I said girl talk…" I huffed and widened my stride to keep up with her. "I think something's wrong with me and it's not cyclical."

"What do you mean something's wrong with you?" Sarah stopped in her tracks and stared at me, but I yanked on her arm and pulled her forward.

We'd almost reached the pickup and a semblance of privacy. The inside of the truck's cab was the closest I would ever get to a soundproofed room.

"Come on. I'll feel better talking about it when we're inside the truck." I let go of her hand and hopped into the driver's side.

Galen's scent enveloped me when I settled into his seat. I closed my eyes and savored the way the rich, earthy tones of his cologne blended with the natural musk of his wolf. But instead of the comfort that normally brought me, I felt anxious and afraid.

Afraid he'd find out I was damaged goods and toss me out of his life and the pack.

"Ugh, I thought you said it wasn't cyclical. If this is a mating thing… I wasn't kidding when I said romance isn't my thing." Sarah shut the passenger door, twisted in her seat to face me, and rested her head back against the window.

"What about physical changes that have nothing to do with body chemistry or being a shifter? Is that one of your things?" I snapped, misdirecting my anger and frustration at my friend instead of where it belonged—with myself.

"What kind of changes? Like a glamour?" Sarah sounded skeptical, as if she'd already guessed a temporary disguise wasn't what I meant.

Although, that gave me an idea and depending on how our conversation went, a glamour might be just what the doctor ordered.

"No, but we might come back to that." I held up my hand to stave off another prodding question from Sarah. "I change when I shift. My wolf is... different."

I wanted to gauge her reaction and get a feel for how bad my situation was before spilling all the details.

"Wait." She held up her index finger and shushed me when I opened my mouth to say something else.

Sarah closed her eyes, inhaled a deep breath through her nose and then blew it out through her mouth. She muttered something in Latin, repeated it three times, praising and thanking the Goddess between each recitation. The air crackled with static electricity like clothes out of the dryer with no fabric softener. After an audible pop, Sarah's eyes flew open.

"Okay, you can talk now." She noted my pinched expression and smiled, while elaborating on the spell she'd performed. "You wanted privacy, right? Well, you got it. Now, what kind of changes to your wolf are you talking about? I assume you don't mean a thicker, shinier coat?"

I loved being a wolf. It was as much a part of me as my strawberry blonde hair or any other physical or psychological attribute, but sometimes I envied the witches' magical abilities.

"My eyes turn red." I blurted out the truth, unable to hold it back any longer.

"Red?" Sarah parroted, apprehension heavy in her voice. "Only when you shift?"

"Right, only when I shift." I nodded, reaffirming my answer.

"Your whole eye? Like in a low budget horror movie or the

actual pigmentation of the iris?" Sarah leaned forward and peered into my eyes as if the answer lay there.

"The iris turns red." I groaned, feeling even more like a freak of nature than I already had thanks to her horror movie analogy.

"Hmm." She propped her elbows on her knees and rested her face in her hands.

The silence stretched on for what felt like an eternity as she mulled over what I'd said.

"You're really freaking me out, Sarah," I told her, when I couldn't stand the wait any longer.

"Sorry, I just..." She sat up, raised her hands and let them drop back into her lap. "I have no idea why that would happen. I mean, I'm a witch so I have a pretty good understanding of science, and how things work, but I'm not a biologist. And I'm not a shifter. Why haven't you talked to Galen about this?"

"How do you know I haven't?" I sounded defeated even to my own ears and I hated it.

"Umm, wild guess?" She shrugged and made a sweeping gesture with her hand. "Or it could be because we're sitting inside his truck surrounded by a magical sound barrier."

The last few weeks had been a series of kicks in the teeth. I never understood why people said things like, you're never given more than you can handle. As if that was somehow a comfort when the universe continued to pile shit on.

I'd never been a defeatist, and always thought I had a pretty positive attitude, with a knack for finding the good in any bad situation. But I struggled to find the silver lining in the storm cloud my life had become in such a short time. I'd been dumped, shamed, exiled, lost my father, been demon marked, and apparently now I'd turned into a freak of nature.

I forced myself to think positively and clung to the slivers of hope I could muster like a lifeline.

I'd also been taken in by a new pack, met Galen who put my

ex to shame in both the looks and personality department, found comfort in my friendship with Max which helped cope with the loss of my dad and had made a new friend in Sarah.

A friend that I trusted and whose help I needed more than anything.

"I haven't told him," I conceded with a sigh. "I don't know what it means and if I can't explain it, I'll just be giving him one more thing to worry about. With everything else going on—"

"Did it occur to you that your eyes changing color might be connected to everything going on?" Sarah held my face in her hands and used her thumbs and forefingers to stretch my eyes open. "Look up and to the left."

"Of course, I thought about that, and it probably is but I need to know why." I rolled my eyes up and to the left, fixating on a small speck of dirt on the headliner. "What's the point of making him stress out over something he can't fix?"

"And you stressing out over it alone is better how, exactly?" She stretched my eyes open wider. "Now look to the right."

"He needs to focus on the Northwood pack and the demon attacks."

"And what if a demon is attacking you?" She let go of my face and leaned back against the window again.

"Is that what you think is happening? The demon who marked me is attacking me from the inside out?" I blinked and rubbed my eyes until the dryness went away.

"I don't know. Maybe."

"You think I'm what? Possessed?" I finally put into words what I was really worried about. I fell back against the seat and stared out the window. "You can fix me though, right?"

"I'm not even sure if that's what's wrong with you, Talia." Sarah scrubbed her face with her hands and combed her fingers through her unruly red hair. "Magic isn't a cure all. I need to know what the problem is before I can create a spell to fix it. Otherwise, it's dangerous."

"How dangerous?" The negative side effects of playing with magic had to be pretty severe before I ruled them out.

"Like the wrong spell could kill you." Sarah crossed her arms over her chest and shook her head. "Magic isn't something you just mess around with, Talia. I'm not a dabbler. I'm a serious practitioner and I could be thrown out of the coven if I caused harm with one of my spells."

Been there, done that, got the tee shirt. I wouldn't have wished banishment on my worst enemy. Never mind my friend.

"So, what am I supposed to do? And please, don't tell me to tell Galen the truth. That's like my last resort."

"I think you hit last resort when your eyes inexplicably turned red." Sarah unfolded her arms and unfastened one of the thin silver bangle bracelets she wore around her wrist. "Here, take this."

"Um, shifter, remember?"

"What? The silver?" She held the bracelet in front of me. A small, smooth orb with swirls of color like an aurora borealis dangled from the bangle. "I thought that was a myth."

"It is." I offered a meager smile, laughing as I dodged her swatting hand. "I'm sorry. This is all so... I just needed to lighten things up."

"I can't believe I fell for that." Sarah rolled her eyes, and the hint of a smile curved the corners of her mouth despite her best effort to appear annoyed.

"What kind of stone is that? I don't think I've ever seen it before."

"Labradorite." Sarah hooked the bracelet around my wrist. "It's a transformation stone and really powerful. So, be careful with it, okay?"

A field of light brown freckles dotted her nose and cheeks.

Sarah's smile grew in tandem with my widening eyes. The bangle was a glamour and the stone its source of magical power.

"This will hide my eyes?" I pinched the multicolored sphere between my thumb and index finger. It was cool to the touch and hummed with energy.

"If that's your intent, then yes. As long as you're wearing it, no one will see any physical attribute you don't want them to." She knew what my intentions were, but I appreciated the instructions. "The bracelet has to be in contact with your skin. The glamour is broken if you take it off."

"But my eyes only turn red when I'm a wolf. I can't wear this when I shift. It might not survive the change."

"I know, but it's the best I've got and if your condition gets worse..." Sarah trailed off.

"I'll have something to hide behind when I'm not a wolf," I said, filling in the blanks.

"Galen's coming." Sarah snapped her fingers, breaking her spell and the wall of silence she'd built around us.

My ears popped when the magic dispersed back into the earth.

"Hey, I hate to interrupt and cut into girl talk time." Galen rapped his knuckles on the driver's window. "But I need to talk to Talia. It's important."

"How long does he think we've been in here?" I asked, confused by Galen's comment.

He hadn't cut anything short. We'd run over. Sarah and I had to have been in the truck for at least twenty minutes.

"He thinks we just left." Sarah wore a satisfied smirk. "What? I knew whatever you needed to talk about was going to take longer than a couple of minutes, so I built a time buffer into the spell."

"It's a good thing you're on our side, because if you ever decided to use that brain of yours for evil we'd be in big trouble." I gave Sarah a hug and whispered my thanks in her ear before she hopped out of the truck.

Galen climbed in behind the wheel as I slid over the console and into the passenger seat.

"Sorry, I know you need a friend, someone to confide in. I wouldn't have interrupted unless it was an emergency."

My brain struggled to process the three-hundred-and-sixty-degree turn in his attitude. He'd been upset with me, and for good reason. I'd put myself and Theo in jeopardy. Understanding why I made that choice didn't mean he had to like it.

And then there was the secret he knew I was keeping from him.

"I, uh, I can be a little overbearing sometimes." Galen shifted in his seat to face me and rested his elbow on the console. "I don't mean to be. I care about you, Talia. I hope you know that, and I want you to have someone to talk to. If you need that person to be Sarah right now, that's okay. But I'm a good listener. Just throwing that out there in case you change your mind."

"Thank you. That means a lot to me, and I know it may not seem like it right now, but I care about you too. So much." I bit the inside of my mouth hard enough to draw blood to keep the truth from spilling out.

I wanted to tell him everything. But I wanted to keep him in my life even more. Which is why I couldn't tell him, not until I knew what was wrong with me.

STILL, if I continued to push him away, Galen would eventually stop pushing back and I would lose him for sure.

An eligible Alpha didn't need to wait around for a woman to decide if she wanted to be his mate. Beautiful women lined up for an opportunity a wolf like Galen could provide. Money, power and security were all powerful aphrodisiacs in their own right.

Add his rugged good looks and incredible physique into the

equation and the answer was simple. A woman had to be out of her mind to let Galen slip away.

I may not have been in my right mind, but I wasn't crazy either. I had every hope of never letting him go.

Galen held out his hand. I laced my fingers through his and brought them to my mouth, brushing the barest hint of a kiss across his knuckles.

"So, what happened? What's the emergency?" I asked, still holding his hand.

"A nationwide Alpha summit has been called to discuss the demon attacks. I'd really like to have you by my side."

"I'd be honored." I ignored my brain, throwing logic and caution out the window and listened to my heart.

With any luck it wouldn't get broken.

CHAPTER 6

GALEN

A mandatory summit of Alphas. It had been years since a meeting of that magnitude had been called. I couldn't have been more than five or six years old when my father attended the last Alpha summit.

He wasn't the same man when he came home.

He still loved and cared for me, and for the pack, but whatever happened during that summit changed him. I saw the shadows in his eyes. The experience haunted him.

I'd been fortunate to have avoided attending one of the annual meetings. My father was Alpha. His presence was required, not mine. He left me in charge while he was gone. Which was fine by me.

I preferred the pack over politics, but if there was ever a time to gather the troops, it was on the verge of a full-scale war with an army of demons.

The coalition that handled issues involving the packs on a national level held an annual conference for Alphas to come and air their grievances, ask for assistance with expansions and form new alliances.

The laws that affected a wolf's daily life were left to the packs and varied by Alpha. Some were tolerant, some were tyrants, but most fell somewhere in the middle like my father. Firm but fair. Respected and unchallenged by their packs.

As long as an Alpha and their pack stayed out of the headlines, they were left to themselves without any interference by the coalition.

When the coalition chose to take up an issue and involve themselves and all of the packs nationwide, it better be for a damned good reason.

Because it was impossible to get everyone to agree on anything.

Which is why I hated politics. It took too long, and nothing got done. The time they spent arguing over what to do and when to do it could have been spent fixing the problem.

The demons forced the coalition to act when they turned their attention to humans.

Each Alpha was permitted two Betas to attend with them. I'd asked Talia to come with me. I wanted her perspective on the Alpha meetings, and I couldn't imagine leaving her behind. It wasn't just about her safety anymore. I felt better when I was around her.

Even when we weren't getting along, I still wanted to be near her.

As for the third member of our party, Theo was my best option. He'd witnessed the last attack and helped Talia save a witch's life. If any of my Betas had something to offer during a summit on demon attacks, it would be him.

Talia and Theo had hit it off from the start and acted more like brother and sister than two people who'd only known each other a few weeks. If I hadn't known better, I would have assumed they'd grown up together. She was so comfortable around him and that was an added bonus.

There was no doubt the summit would test us. We needed to present a show of strength and unity.

We went straight from the coven's encampment to the meeting house where all three of my Betas were waiting. I'd leaned on them heavily as my father's health declined and I stepped into the role of acting Alpha. My absence would only add to their mounting responsibilities, but there wasn't anyone else I could trust with the pack while I was gone.

"What's going on?" Markus asked in lieu of a greeting. He wasn't one to mince words and cut right to the chase as usual. "You sounded stressed out on the phone. Was there another attack?"

"No, worse." I held the door for Talia, pulling it closed once she'd entered the room.

"There's something worse than a demon attack?" Darius had been on security detail with David who was forced to bring him along or risk missing out on our meeting.

I wasn't entirely comfortable with Darius's presence or discussing the summit in front of him. He had ingratiated himself into the pack, but that didn't mean I trusted him. Still, I was short on time and people I could trust. Since they were all in the same room as Darius, I was left with little choice but to talk business.

"A national summit has been called to deal with the demon attacks." I pulled out my phone and opened up the calendar app. "We leave as soon as we're packed and will be gone for three days."

"We?" Markus's gaze flicked from me to Talia and back again. One corner of his mouth upturned. The grin matched the mischievous look in his eyes. "I'm sure Talia will love the ranch. It's beautiful this time of year."

"I doubt we'll have a chance to see that much of it." I closed my eyes and groaned; worried my poor choice of words would lead to Talia or myself being the butt of several jokes before the night was out. "Theo's coming too."

Especially when I continued to make it worse.

"Well, that's a shame." Markus winked but spared our pride from a ribbing. "Talia, if you get some free time outside of the summit's itinerary, go for a run. The sky feels like it goes on forever. There's nothing like it."

"I went once when I was a little girl. It was a long time ago, after my mother died. My father was close to the Alpha. Not the piece of shit running the Northwood pack now, the one before. Maddox's grandfather." Talia fidgeted with the bracelet on her wrist. "Anyway, no one would watch me. So, I tagged along. I don't remember much from the trip, but I do remember thinking how pretty it was."

That was the first time she'd mentioned having been to the ranch. Talia and I hadn't been together—if we even considered together—long enough to know each other's histories. But I wanted to. I wanted to know everything about her. What made her tick, what made her think and feel the way she did.

I also wanted to pull her into my arms and comfort her, tell her everything would be okay. While most of the stories she'd shared with me hadn't been tragic, few of them had been happy. They reminded me that she didn't have the same upbringing in a pack that I did.

Talia deserved happiness and I wanted to be the one to give that to her.

"You said you're taking Theo with you?" David's gaze was fixed on Talia despite his question being directed at me.

I recognized the haunted look in his eyes. It was the same look in Talia's eyes when she spoke about her parents and the same look in mine when I thought about Jessie. Some losses are so great that we never get over them. All we can do is make room for the pain in our hearts.

"Yeah." I scratched at the stubble sprouting along my jaw and cleared my throat a couple of times. "That's why I called you guys here, to go over who's doing what while I'm gone."

"I've got pack operations covered." David motioned with his hand, his pointer finger slightly extended. "And I'll make arrangements for someone with medical training to check in on your dad. We've got enough nurses and EMTs in the pack. It should be easy to put a rotation together and I'll crash on the couch at his place at night."

"I'm on security. The wards are holding, but I'll keep in contact with Marguerite while you're away, maybe talk with her about the coven setting up a border check of their own that coincides with ours." Markus pulled out his phone, muttering out loud as he jotted down a few ideas to implement his plan. "With demons and the Northwood pack attacking, we could use witches and wolves on patrol anyway."

"I agree." I should have known a meeting wasn't necessary. Markus and David stepped right into the roles I would have assigned them without asking or hesitation. The pack was in good hands.

"Looks like I get to go on vacation. I guess I'll go pack." Theo smiled at Markus and David, waving to them both while whistling his way out the door. "If you suckers need me, I'll be at the spa getting a massage. Don't work too hard, boys."

"There's a spa?" David had yet to visit the ranch. Had the circumstances been different, I would have asked him to serve as my Beta for the summit.

Hell, I would have sent him in my stead if I could have.

"Don't worry." Markus gave David a firm pat on the back. "We've got three days to come up with some grueling tasks that only Theo can do when he gets home. Preferably one involving intense physical labor."

"What about me?" Darius spoke up for the first time, drawing all eyes toward him. "I can go with you. Sounds like Markus and David have everything covered here. A national summit on demons is a big deal. You're going to need another wolf with you."

"I appreciate the offer, but each Alpha is only permitted two wolves to accompany them. Keeps tensions down. Less chance for skirmishes to break out. Besides, I could really use your help at the bar while I'm gone."

That was a lie.

I didn't appreciate Darius's offer; I was suspicious of it. The longer he stayed in the pack, the more skeptical I became of his arrival and intentions. Maybe he was a spy for the Northwood pack. Or worse, an assassin waiting for the right moment to strike.

Either way, I didn't trust him, and I didn't want him anywhere near the summit.

One of the perks about being an Alpha was that the dominance we held over our pack members made it more difficult for them to know when we weren't telling the truth. It wasn't impossible to sniff out a lie, but most wolves couldn't.

Markus, on the other hand, could.

Of course, as one of my Betas and closest friends he had an advantage. He knew my tells. Which is why I refused to play poker with him.

Markus arched a quizzical brow, asking for more information without uttering a word. I gave a subtle shake of my head, staving off any questions until later. If Darius was up to something I didn't want to risk tipping him off before I figured out what it was.

"Just two?" Darius scoffed at the number of wolves from each pack permitted to attend the summit. "You'd think with all the demons running around they'd want more of us around. That's a lot of important people all in one place. I mean, what if the demons attack the summit?"

He raised a valid point. Attacking the summit was a smart move and one I hoped the council had taken into consideration.

It also raised an interesting question.

I couldn't help but wonder if Darius knew something about the demon attacks. Had he heard something and failed to share it with the rest of us? Was he waiting until an opportune time presented itself? One that benefited him and his position in the pack.

"The ranch is fortified, and the council has security. They won't be taking any chances."

Summit security measures were not something I would have elaborated on with anyone other than my Betas. So why did I feel the need to stress that fact with him?

With all the trouble we'd had with the demons and witches, there hadn't been time to vet Darius properly. That wasn't protocol and it was out of character for me. I liked to know who I was dealing with and what they were capable of.

Usually, I left nothing to chance when it came to new members. The wrong choice for a new packmate could lead to disaster for the pack.

And yet, I rolled the dice anyway.

In my defense, we had our hands full. To say I was desperate for new blood in the pack to grow our ranks would have been a massive understatement.

From the moment Darius showed up in town, he'd fit right in and even helped out at the bar. He just slid right into place. He seemed too good to be true even then.

My father always said, if something looks too good to be true, then you know that it isn't good.

I knew the risks and took a chance. Something I had done too much of in recent weeks. Talia was the only risk that I thought would have paid off and I found myself questioning that decision as well.

When my father got sick, the pack looked to me to make all the decisions. The change in roles was sudden. I wasn't prepared and in situations like this, where I questioned my own pack, my own feelings, I doubted that I ever would be ready.

I longed for the days when these problems were my father's problems.

"All right, you guys have your orders." I said in lieu of goodbye, chuckling when David gave a mock salute.

"We should probably go. There's a lot to do before we leave for the summit. We both need to pack and I'm sure you want to check in on Max as much as I do." Talia took my hand in hers, laced our fingers together and with a gentle tug, led me toward the door.

"We've got everything covered. Don't worry." Markus clamped his hand on my shoulder and walked Talia out the door.

Don't worry. Easier said than done. As much as I would have liked to follow that advice, there was plenty to worry about and all of it fell on me.

Trouble wasn't just on our doorstep. It had kicked the front door in, and I was the pack's last line of defense.

I just hoped I was the Alpha they needed me to be.

CHAPTER 7
TALIA

Galen had been called to a summit and out of all the wolves, including his three Betas, he wanted me to go with him.

And not just because he was concerned I'd get into trouble while he was gone.

There was no doubt in my mind that his concern for my safety was part of it. Galen seemed to think that I was safer with him. The events of the last few weeks proved otherwise.

I'd been attacked and in more fights since joining the Long Claw pack than I had been in my entire life before that. Of course, women had been discouraged from fighting. Our place wasn't on the battlefield—until the Northwood Alpha needed it to be.

My newfound freedom was both terrifying and exhilarating.

Galen gave me the room my wolf and I needed to grow. I never realized what I'd been missing in my life until he showed me what a pack was meant to be—and I realized that I'd been tolerated more than I'd been accepted.

For the first time I felt that I belonged, and I refused to let some demon mark infect me and ruin everything.

Sarah's imbued charm bracelet provided a magical camouflage and bought me some time to figure out what was happening to me. The summit would keep Galen occupied and allow me to continue my search for the answer to my wolf's red eyes.

"It means a lot to me, having you at my side during the summit." Galen spared a glance in my direction before returning his attention to the road. "It's not just about some baser need to protect you. I want you there...with me."

"It means a lot to me too, Galen." I rested my hand, palm up, on the console in an unspoken invitation to connect.

Warmth rushed through my body and my heart raced when he slid his hand over mine and locked our fingers together.

"I know I've been distant lately, Galen. It's not you."

I caught the side-eye and a small tick in his jaw muscle. He didn't believe me. I supposed I hadn't given him much reason.

"Okay, maybe it's a little bit... Or a lot-a-bit, about you." I wasn't ready to give him the whole truth.

But it wasn't a lie either.

He was the reason I put so much distance between us, that I was terrified for anyone to discover the truth about my eyes or what it meant for them to turn red. I was falling for him, and I was terrified of losing him.

That thought scared the hell out of me.

"I was afraid you were going to say that." He moved to pull his hand away, but I clamped down and wouldn't let go.

"You scare me, Galen." I raised our hands to my lips and brushed featherlight kisses across his knuckles. "The way you make me feel... I was engaged, about to be married to my fated mate. I shouldn't feel this way, right? I mean, how is it..."

"Possible? It shouldn't be. At least, not that I've ever heard. But who am I to question Destiny?" Galen's dimple punctuated the mischievous smile on his face.

"Isn't Destiny the same thing as Fate?" I matched his smile with my own.

"Maybe. But what are the odds that I would kidnap the wrong girl?" He flicked his turn signal and steered the truck to the left onto Cypress Lane.

"Huh, when you put it that way, maybe it's Stockholm syndrome and not Destiny at all."

Sarah was sitting on the porch, waiting for us to arrive, when we pulled into the driveway. She hopped up off the concrete steps and bounded down the walkway.

"Did you know she was coming over?" Galen shut off the truck and climbed out of the cab.

"Nope, she never mentioned it." I unbuckled my seatbelt and hopped out.

Sarah sidestepped to give Galen room to pass on the walkway, fell into step beside me and draped her arm over my shoulder.

"Marguerite just finished a new batch of ointments and elixirs for Max. She wanted to make sure his caretakers were fully stocked while you're away at the summit and asked me to drop them off before you left."

"Thanks, Sarah." Galen unlocked the door and held it open for us. "Checking his meds was on my to-do list before we headed out. So, I really appreciate that."

"One less thing for you guys to do." Sarah beamed at him and strolled into the living room. "Need help packing? Happy to lend a hand or two while I'm here."

Max's medicine wasn't the only reason for Sarah's visit. We could have easily picked them up or made arrangements for David to take care of that before we left for the summit. There was something else she wanted to talk to me about and whatever it was, she clearly did not want to say it in front of Galen.

Which meant only one thing. She had information about my eyes.

"I mean, since you're here and we're in a rush to get on the road..." I headed for my room, pausing in the small foyer, and glanced over my shoulder at Galen. "We can help you pack after I'm done if you want?"

"I'm good. We'll only be gone a couple of days and I pack light." Galen smiled as he passed us on the way to Max's room. "Oh, do you have an evening gown?"

"Seriously?" I barked out a bitter laugh.

I left the Northwood pack with whatever I could fit in my suitcases and in the trunk of my car. It wasn't much and did not include formal wear.

"The last gown I bought was white and I left it back at my old house."

"Right." Galen grimaced; his cheeks flushed with obvious embarrassment. "There's a clothing store in the hotel on the ranch. I'm sure they'll have a dress or can have something delivered for you."

"They have a department store?" Sarah's eyes were as wide as saucers. "How big is the hotel?"

"It's more of a reservation than a ranch. The council and their families stay there year-round. There are security staff, hotel staff, and naturalists who maintain the wildlife preserve. It's like a state unto itself. And that's not even including the local pack that lives on the property." Galen shrugged off the size and amount of people on the property as if it was no big deal.

But to a small-town girl from a small pack, it was a huge deal.

What did I know about formal events or politics? A whole lot of nothing. That's what.

"I know this isn't like a real vacation, but I'm kind of jealous. A fancy hotel, fancier clothes." One corner of Sarah's' mouth turned up in a mischievous grin and there was a devilish glint in her eyes. "And, of course, the hotel room. It's a suite, isn't it? With a king size bed, I bet."

"Rooms. There will be multiple rooms," Galen corrected, to my relief.

Just the thought of sharing a room and a bed with him sent my heart racing—and not in the way I would have expected. I wanted Galen. His wolf called to me and mine. That scared the hell out of me.

I'd never felt so woefully unprepared. To say I was inexperienced when it came to sex was the understatement of understatements.

Galen had been in a committed relationship, and I didn't get the impression he was a promise ring sort of guy.

Maddox and I never went on a trip together for business or pleasure. We'd never shared a bedroom, never mind a hotel room, having agreed to wait until our wedding night for anything more intimate than second base.

Knowing we would have separate rooms took the pressure of our trip that I hadn't realized was there until Sarah nudged my ribs with her elbow and winked in my direction.

"I, umm... I should probably go... umm." My gaze traveled the length of Galen's body.

Sarah had planted the idea of Galen and I sharing a room and all the possibilities that went with that into my head and I couldn't think of anything else.

"Pack?" Galen's knowing smile had me questioning how deep the pack bond went and whether or not he could read my mind.

"Yeah, pack."

I grabbed Sarah's hand and fled to my bedroom before Galen noticed the flush of embarrassment heating my cheeks.

"That was mortifying." I closed the door to my room behind us, flattening my back against the wood panel. "Sleeping arrangements hadn't even occurred to me and now it's all I can think about."

"If I was running around with a witch that looked like Galen, it would have been the first thing I thought about." Sarah threw herself onto my bed, giggling like a schoolgirl at a slumber party. "So, you two haven't, you know—"

"No." I rushed to answer before she could finish. "We haven't. I haven't."

"You mean... No." Sarah looked like a fish out of water, her mouth opening and closing a few times before she regained her composure. "But you were engaged."

"We wanted to wait until the honeymoon." I pushed off the door with a sigh and went to the closet in search of my mid-sized, black canvas rolling travel bag. "It seemed sweet and romantic when I was getting married, but now?"

"I'm sorry. I shouldn't have teased you. I didn't know." Sarah apologized and stretched out on the memory foam mattress, her feet dangling off the end of the bed.

"I don't care about that." I brushed off Sarah's assumption. That wasn't the real reason I'd been upset. "It's just, I did everything right, I was the good girl, I waited, and it didn't get me anywhere but tossed out. I feel like I missed out on a lot of my own life because I was living it for someone else."

"Your ex was a first-class jerk." Sarah sat up and swung her legs over the side of the bed. "But you're through with him. He's in the past. Fate must have been wrong about your mate."

That got my full attention. I'd wondered the same thing since I woke up with a throbbing headache on the floor of a small cabin on the edge of Long Claw territory.

"You think so?" I clutched the black, button-down silk blouse, still on its hanger, and rounded on her. "Do you really think Fate could have been wrong about me and Maddox?"

"I think if someone who looked like Galen looked at me the way he does you, I'd be questioning everything about Fate, Destiny, the universe, or whatever you want to call it."

"Maybe you're right. Maddox is behind me, and I need to just let whatever is happening with Galen, happen." I slipped the blouse off its hanger, folded it and set it on top of the other clothes I'd piled into my small suitcase.

It felt good to dump the baggage from my relationship with Maddox and put him where he belonged. Behind me. From that moment on I was moving forward.

Or at least that's what I thought. I should have sent Sarah the memo.

"So umm, Talia? I know your aura is all glowy and you're feeling better right now, but I came here to talk to you."

"I know. I was hoping I might be able to distract you." I picked the laciest bras and panties I owned on the off chance that someone other than myself would see them and tucked them in the suitcase. "I thought if we kept talking about Galen and my virginity, I could get out the door before you had a chance to say anything."

"Clever." Sarah's smile never reached her eyes. "I came here to tell you not to go with Galen to the summit. Something bad is going to happen, I can feel it."

"Between me and Galen?" I looked at the matching sets of undergarments I'd packed in my suitcase and wondered if I should even bother.

"No, that's not what I mean. At least I don't think it is." She held up her hand to stave off my questions. Her gaze narrowed and her face scrunched up. I knew that look. She stopped to take a deeper look at whatever bad omen she felt compelled to warn me about.

I just hoped she was right, and it had nothing to do with me and Galen.

"Don't unpack the lace panties. It's not about you and Galen." Sarah's shoulders drooped and her expression relaxed. "At least not romantically."

"Good." I couldn't help the smile that spread across my face.

I'd gotten pretty good at rolling with the punches over the last few weeks. What was a little more bad news? As long as it wasn't about Galen's feelings for me, or whatever was developing between us, I was sure I could handle it. Because that meant I wouldn't be handling it alone.

Unless it had something to do with my eyes.

"Is it the demon mark? Or whatever it's doing to me?" I was convinced my eyes, and the mark were connected.

They had to be. The timing was just too much of a coincidence, and I didn't really believe in coincidences. There was no other logical explanation for it. If I figured out how to get rid of the demon mark, I was certain my eyes would go back to normal.

But to do that, I needed to tell Galen what was happening.

"I'm going to tell him." I expressed my confidence in the connection with the mark and my eyes and shared my plans to tell Galen everything with Sarah.

She didn't seem as convinced as me.

"I don't know, Talia. It might not even be that. It could be something with the summit, some kind of danger there. Right now, the only thing I know for sure is it's bigger than your love life. And when I say bigger, I mean bigger. This doesn't just feel like a storm coming, it feels like a hurricane bearing down."

"You're quite the harbinger of doom."

I slipped the narrow rectangular black velvet jewelry box that held my mother's diamond pendant and matching earrings into my suitcase and zipped it closed. The stones were small but elegant and, I hoped, a suitable accessory to whatever dress I could find when we went shopping at the hotel store.

"I know." Sarah's deadpan tone and expression sent goosebumps skirting across my skin and raised the hair on the back of my neck and arms. "I really think you should stay here."

"Even if I wanted to stay here, Galen would never go for it." I yanked on the retractable suitcase handle to extend it to its full position and rolled the bag beside the door. "He'll be too worried something will happen to me while he's gone and after what you've said, I would worry something might happen to him."

"That's what I'm trying to tell you, Talia. Something is going to happen." Sarah raked her hands through her hair and combed her fingers through the tangled ends of her wildfire locks. "He has to go to the summit. You don't."

"Sarah, your friendship means the world to me. I don't know what I would do if I didn't have you in my life." I plopped down beside her on my bed. "And I know you're worried. I am too, but—"

"You're going, no matter what I say or do." She picked at a loose thread on the dandelion yellow duvet cover spread over my bed.

"I am."

"That bracelet isn't going to protect you from whatever is coming." She pulled the thread on the duvet, snapping it free from the length still stitched to the soft cotton fabric, and let the broken piece fall to the floor.

Sarah was a powerful witch, and I valued her advice. It was a shame I couldn't take it.

CHAPTER 8

GALEN

Talia went straight to her room with Sarah in tow to start packing as soon as we got home. She seemed excited about joining me on the trip to Montana. The circumstances could have been better, but I hoped the time together would bring us closer.

"Almost ready?" I called out, glancing at my watch to make sure we stayed on schedule.

"Ten more minutes. Fifteen tops," Talia shouted back from her room.

We had a long drive and I still needed to pick up Theo before we left. I also needed to swing by the bar to make sure things were under control and grab a few things from my apartment above the bar. But we could spare a few extra minutes.

There was one other thing I needed to do before we got on the road—seek my father's advice.

I moved with purpose, eager to speak with him, only to hit the brakes when the soft sounds of snoring reached me through his bedroom door. As much as I hated to wake him, I knew he'd be upset if I didn't.

"Dad." With a soft knock, I turned the doorknob and let myself in. "Hey, I'm sorry to wake you, but the council called an all-Alpha summit."

"Mandatory?" My father rubbed the sleep from his eyes, pushed himself up to a seated position and leaned back against the headboard.

It pained me to watch him deteriorate before my eyes with no medical explanation or cure. He'd been a picture of health and a strong leader every day of his life and then one day he just wasn't.

It should have been him going to the summit. Not me.

"Galen, I can feel the stress radiating off you. Bring the chair over here and sit down." He crooked a finger at the ladderback chair in the corner of the room. "There, now tell me what's on your mind."

"Apart from the obvious?" I laughed off the budding stress and anxiety of representing the Long Claw pack at a national meeting and settled into the chair at my father's bedside.

"The obvious is as good a place to start as any." My dad reached for the glass of water on a small rolling tray.

"Well, for starters, you should be the one going to this meeting. You're still the Alpha, Dad." I rested my elbows on my knees and propped my head in my hands with a defeated sigh. "What if I'm not cut out for this? What if I screw up on the national stage?"

"The summit is the perfect time and place for you to officially assume control of the pack." He curled his knobby fingers into a ball and coughed into his fist. "You're my son, which means you are meant for this."

"How can you be so sure?" I used the tips of my fingers to massage my temples and stave off the headache barreling toward me like a runaway train. "Everything has fallen apart since you got sick."

"And you think that's your fault?" His eyes were clouded with a milky white film, but his gaze pierced my soul, nonetheless.

"Only an idiot would believe that, and I didn't raise an idiot, did I?"

"No, Dad. You didn't."

"That's what I thought. Now, for the slightly less obvious." My dad chuckled, covering his mouth with his fist when the laughter turned into another coughing fit.

He swatted my hand away when I reached for his oxygen mask.

"Tell me about Talia. What's going on with you two?"

Once he set me on the path of conversation he wanted to follow, he hooked the elastic straps of the clear plastic mask behind his ears, fixed it over his nose and mouth and took a deep breath of the oxygen that pumped from the tank, through the tubing and into his lungs.

I hated seeing him like that, but I hated leaving him alone even more.

The pack would look after him. David would make sure of that. A rotation of medical care would be set up. Some of the families in the pack would drop off meals. I was grateful for their help, but it wasn't the same as having Talia to look after him.

She'd taken a liking to him from the start and their friendship grew into something akin to a father-daughter relationship.

"You mean besides the fact that she's driving me crazy?"

"The best women usually do." He lowered the oxygen mask, hooking it around his chin. It muffled his words and he refused to wear it for long. "But there's something else. Something's troubling her and she won't talk to me about it."

"Yeah, me either," I grumbled, wringing my hands in my lap. "I don't know what to do or say to make her trust me enough to open up, but if she won't, how can I trust her?"

"Trust is a two-way street, son. So is communication."

"You don't have to tell me." I jabbed my index finger toward my chest. "I'm the one doing all the talking."

"You can't do much listening, Galen, if you're always the one talking."

"Dad, cut the guidance counselor crap," I snapped at him, and then apologized the instant the words left my mouth.

He was too frail to be a punching bag and hadn't done anything for me to take my frustration out on him.

"It's all right, son. She's under your skin, gets you worked up. That's a good thing. I haven't seen you like this around a woman since—"

"Since Jessie." I finished for him.

And that was part of the problem.

I'd carried Jessie's ghost around in my heart for so long, wearing the guilt of her death like a badge of honor, that I'd forgotten what falling in love felt like.

It was amazing, wondrous, and absolutely terrifying.

"Things haven't always been easy for you. The son of an Alpha. Losing your first love, your mate, the way you did. But when things were at their worst you had people to fall back on. You had me. You had your pack."

"And I'm grateful for that, Dad. I want to be that for Talia, but she won't let me. Maybe I'm wrong. Maybe she doesn't feel the same way about me. Maybe she isn't who she says she is and she's still with Maddox."

"That's a lot of maybes, Galen." Light tremors shook his hands as he smoothed the blanket. "Let's focus on the known instead of the unknown. So, what do we know? We know you care about her, and we know she cares about you. I've seen the way she looks at you, the way she talks about you when you're not around. That girl thinks you hung the moon."

"Dad—"

"Nope. You came in here for my advice and you're going to get it. Talia lost both her parents and then her pack. They disowned her, tossed her out into the world to fend for herself. She has as many reasons not to trust people as you, or anyone else. Hell, probably more. You think about that the next time you doubt her motives—or your feelings for her."

"Do you ever get tired of being right?" I leaned back in the chair with a meager smile on my face and crossed my arms over my chest.

"Nope." His body shook with the laughter he held back to prevent another coughing fit. "You wouldn't come to see me nearly as much if I were wrong."

"You know that's a lie." I glanced at my watch. "I better check on Talia and see if she's ready to go."

"This trip isn't just about the summit. It's a chance for you and Talia. So, don't blow it. I like having her around."

"Me too, Dad. Me too." I pushed myself up and out of the chair, crossed the room and flicked the light switch on my way out the door. "Get some rest. I'll see you in a couple of days."

Talia sat on the couch in the living room, scrolling through something on her phone while she waited for me. Her suitcase was by the front door, and I hadn't even started packing.

"Ready?" I fished my keys out of my front jeans pocket and grabbed the suitcase handle.

"You're not even packed." Talia tossed her phone in her messenger bag, slipped the strap over her shoulder and across her chest, and met me at the door.

"I need to swing by the bar and check in with the staff before we go. I'll grab what I need from my apartment while we're there."

"I'll drive." She snatched the keys out of my hand and sprinted out the door.

Theo was seated at the bar, knocking back one beer and ordering his second by the time we rolled in. Terri, my bartender and occasional bouncer, used the edge of the old wooden counter to snap off the metal cap and set the glass bottle in front of Theo.

Talia and I sidled up to the bar, taking seats on either side of my Beta. I signaled for Terri to come back around after he finished with another customer.

"What can I get you?" Terri pulled two wafer-thin cork coasters from under the counter and set them on the bar top in front of me and Talia.

"Nothing for me." I leaned on the bar and peered around Theo for a better look at Talia. "Order whatever you'd like. It's on me. I won't be long."

"If I knew you were picking up the tab, I'd have ordered an appetizer." Theo tipped his beer in salute.

"He pays double."

I filled Terri in on as many of the details of my trip as I could. Which wasn't much. The council members weren't known for their altruism. Their involvement in the demon attacks wasn't for the sake of humans or witches.

They only cared about wolves.

The summit was pack business. The bar had been spared in the latest demon attacks on the town and in the turf war with the Northwood pack. I wouldn't risk my staff by oversharing.

"Darius offered to pitch in again. So, if you need any help, give him a call." I rapped my knuckles on the bar top and slid off my stool. "And you know how to get a hold of me if there's any trouble."

"No worries, boss." Terri tucked a white microfiber hand towel in the black apron fastened around his waist. "We've got things covered here."

"Like always."

My selective hiring process for bar staff had paid off. Terri and the rest of the crew held down the fort whenever I wasn't around. Which, in the last few weeks, had been more often than not.

I'd considered selling the bar on more than one occasion. Successful small businesses needed hands-on owners. If I became Alpha, I would have even less time to run the bar. Running off to yet another pack emergency, only served to prove my point.

And yet, I couldn't bring myself to sell it.

The bar was mine. It didn't belong to the pack. It was an achievement that I had accomplished outside of my father's shadow. The decisions that I made for the business weren't life or death either. No one would die if I opted for an IPA over a dark ale.

But the pack? Lives hung in the balance with every choice I made.

To fight or not to fight. That was the question. One that seemed to plague Alphas the world over. Or at least, those attending the summit.

Myself included.

The bar was an escape. A break from the weight of the responsibilities I felt stepping into my father's shoes and the reality that I would follow those footsteps sooner rather than later.

But it looked like my break was over.

The summit was a stark reminder of who and what I was—the son of an Alpha. They had come to depend on me the same way they depended on my father. I was the future of the Long Claw pack. They needed me.

And I realized just how much I needed them.

Everything was riding on the summit. I couldn't let them down. I wouldn't let them down. I would stand before the council, representing the Long Claw pack, and be the Alpha they deserved.

CHAPTER 9
TALIA

My legs fell asleep an hour or two into the drive. If only my brain could have done the same. I'd planned to close my eyes and catch up on some sleep during the trip, but whenever I was about to doze off, my mind raced again.

The highlight reel played out one embarrassing scenario after another of me during the summit until I became a live wire of nervous energy.

Galen called Theo, who'd driven his own car and followed behind us, to announce a pit stop. He rerouted the GPS to the nearest gas station. I was out of the truck, stretching my legs before he killed the engine.

"Would you mind grabbing me a coffee and something to eat from inside? I'm starving." Galen tossed his black leather wallet over the roof of the car.

"Sure thing." I grabbed a couple of twenties from inside the billfold and slid the wallet back. "What are you in the mood for? Sweet, salty?"

"Protein bars would be good and whatever you want." He slid a credit card into the pump and punched a few buttons on the small computer screen. "And before you say you're not hungry, the opening ceremony at these things takes forever. It'll be a while before we can grab a meal."

I couldn't recall the last thing I ate or the last time I felt hungry. The constant state of stress I'd been living in had wreaked havoc on my appetite. My jeans were a little looser, and I'd added a notch to one of my favorite belts.

The nonexistent migraines I used as my cover for avoiding events that required me to shift in front of Galen or the pack, took the blame for my suppressed appetite as well. The rising anxiety over the course of the trip hadn't increased my desire for food, but Galen was right. I needed to eat something.

The last thing I needed was to draw attention to myself during the opening ceremony with a rumbling stomach or worse, by passing out.

I unloaded a small shopping basket with various granola bars, protein and meal replacement bars, two large black coffees for the guys and a vitamin infused water for me, onto the counter. Thirty-odd dollars later I was back in the truck, and we were on the road once again.

With another two hours of the trip remaining, I tugged on my seatbelt, readjusted my position on the seat and rested my head against the window in the hopes of a little nap before we arrived.

"Talia." Galen rubbed his hand up and down my arm. "We're here. Time to wake up."

"Already?" It felt like I had just closed my eyes.

"You've been snoring since we left the gas station." Galen teased before unbuckling his seatbelt and opening the driver's door.

"I don't snore," I protested and wiped my hand over my mouth to check the corners for any hints of drool.

"No, of course you don't."

His retort shattered any illusions that I may have had about resembling a fairytale princess under a spell while I slept. Mortified, I climbed out of the truck in silence and walked around to the back for my suitcase.

The ranch didn't look like much of a ranch. At least not like any I'd seen before. Albeit my only experience with ranching had been what I'd seen on TV or in the movies. Still, there were no livestock, stables, or ranch hands in sight.

What it lacked in reenacted frontier life, it more than made up for in a panoramic view of Montana's stunning landscape. Log cabins dotted the plains and the Ponderosa Pine-covered hills that bordered the council grounds.

"Here, let me get that."

Galen came around, slung the strap to his duffle bag over his shoulder and took my suitcase, wheeling it behind him as he headed for a small kiosk and a young man in a deep navy-blue uniform stationed behind it.

He exchanged the truck keys for a ticket stub and led the way inside a sprawling log cabin filled with people who I assumed were attending the summit as well. A line in front of a counter with a sign indicating guest services snaked through the lobby and stopped a couple of feet from the entrance.

From what I read on the information sheet handed to us by a staff member on entry, the main lodge housed two banquet halls, conference rooms, a dining hall, lounge, and games room. Guests were provided with fully enclosed UTV transportation to and from their lodgings and other ranch amenities.

The ranch was available for private pack meetings, and ceremonies when not in use for national pack or council business.

We were directed to the queue, where an efficient staff tended to dozens of guests, sorting rooms and reservations, until finally it was Galen's turn at the counter.

"Let me see." The fair-haired woman behind the counter, whose name tag read Linda, Head of Guest Services, typed Galen's name into their booking system. "You said Long Claw pack, right?"

"Yes, that's right." Galen grabbed a brochure and menu from a clear plastic holder on the countertop and handed them to me.

"Ah, there you are." Linda tapped the screen with her index finger, reached under the counter and produced an old-fashioned room key complete with a plastic tag that dangled from the keyring. "You'll be in the Harrier House. The small barn is converted into two efficiencies, each with a king-sized bed. There is also a shared porch and hot tub, and of course, breathtaking views of Rock Creek."

"There's only one bed? You're such a blanket hog. I guess we'll just have to spoon." Theo strolled across the lobby, sidled up to the counter and winked at Linda. "Shoot, I didn't pack any pajamas."

"Is there a pullout sofa in one of the rooms or a cot that could be brought out to the cabin?" Galen palmed the key and hitched the strap of his bag higher up on his shoulder.

"I'm sorry, sir." She hid her smile behind her hand and cleared her throat. "My apologies. As I'm sure you can imagine, we are completely booked for the summit. Due to the overwhelming response to the council's call for the summit, we had to limit the number of rooms for each pack."

"I see." Galen side-eyed Theo. "If a room should become available, you'll let us know?"

"Of course. You'll be the first to hear of any cancellations." Linda dipped down behind the counter and popped up seconds later with another key in her hand, which she proceeded to hand over to Theo. "Perhaps, the lovely lady accompanying you could suggest a more suitable sleeping arrangement?"

"If it's the lady's choice, I already know who she'll pick. Besides, I have a thing for redheads." Theo slathered on a thick layer of charm and went to make his move. "I don't suppose you're—"

"I'm flattered. But the ranch frowns upon the staff fraternizing with guests during summits."

"Frowns upon, but not forbids, right?" Theo pressed his luck, but Linda held her ground and politely asked for a rain check that we all knew she wouldn't cash. "You know where to find me if you change your mind."

"I do, yes." Linda wished us well and went about her business, calling the next Alpha and his entourage up to the counter.

"I mean, day-uumm. Am I right?" Theo spared a quick glance over his shoulder to see if Linda was watching him.

She wasn't.

"Remind me why I brought you again?" Galen shook his head, clapped his hand on Theo's shoulder and steered us back to the lobby entrance. "Come on. We need to get settled in our rooms before the opening ceremony."

"It's a wonder you're still single," I teased, falling in step with Galen and Theo.

"Right?" Theo replied, holding the door for us.

A bellhop loaded our bags onto the back of a UTV and gave us directions to the Harrier House cabin.

Linda hadn't exaggerated about the breathtaking views. The creek's crystal-clear water carved its way through the lush green plain. The air was clean, crisp, and smelled like the end of autumn. The last of the leaves had fallen. Winter was coming and the countryside would be blanketed with snow.

Harrier House was an old barn converted into two efficiencies —called the loft and the stable. The former was the smaller of the two rooms.

"I call top bunk." Theo hopped off the utility vehicle that resembled a toy truck and grabbed his duffle bag.

"You haven't even seen inside." Galen came around to my side of the UTV and offered a supportive hand as I climbed out. "One of the rooms might be better equipped to sleep two."

"I'm going to check out the first floor." I grabbed the handle of my suitcase and dragged it behind me.

The wheels created two uneven tracks as they sank into the pea gravel walkway that led up to the double barn doors. The first floor had an open floor plan and was decorated in a rustic combination of farmhouse chic and midwestern ranch. The windows updated in the resort renovations added to the openness of the space and brought the outside in.

There was a small seating area with a brown leather loveseat worn to perfection and two matching oversized armchairs nestled in front of a wood burning fireplace. Had I known, I would have packed a book or two to curl up with—though I doubted I would have time to read them.

The space had everything I needed. Coffee pot, snack basket, and mini bar. A hot tub and two Adirondack rockers sat on the front porch. But it was the porcelain claw-footed soaker tub seated near a wall of windows that overlooked the creek with a perfect view of the sky that sealed the deal.

The boys could have the loft. I didn't care.

"So, the upstairs loft is a lot smaller and really outfitted for one person." Galen popped his head in the door and gave the first-floor efficiency a once over. "Would you consider swapping?"

"Absolutely not. Do you see that?" I pointed to the soaker tub. "I am going to soak until I prune, every chance I get. But there is a loveseat and you're welcome to bunk with me instead. If you want."

The words were out of my mouth before I realized what I'd said.

My heart raced and my hands went clammy. I had just offered to share a room, not a bed, with Galen. Still, spending every night in close proximity with a hot blooded, sexy-as-hell Alpha would send my wolf and the crush I'd developed for him into hyperdrive.

I was inexperienced and worried that if things progressed—and I was pretty certain I wanted them to—Galen would be disappointed. It was like performance anxiety without ever having performed.

But that wasn't the worst of my problems.

I had just made it that much more difficult to keep my eyes hidden by inviting the one person most likely to notice to spend more time with me. I hoped like hell that Sarah's charm bracelet held out over the course of the summit.

"Stay with you? Yeah, sure." Galen straightened, shoulders back and chest puffed, with bright eyes and a lopsided grin on his face. "I'll just... let me go grab my bag and let Theo know he's got the loft to himself."

Galen seemed to share my nervous excitement about sharing a room. I was determined not to force it. Whatever happened would happen naturally.

Even a perfect plan could end in disaster. My life had already been proof enough of that. Had things worked out like I'd planned, I would have been back in the Northwood pack, married, and awaiting Maddox's return from the summit.

Maybe Fate had second thoughts about my mate. I sure as hell did. Maddox had a long way to fall from the ivory tower I'd put him in. It's a wonder he survived the fall. Our engagement hadn't.

The fallout of my relationship with Maddox had turned out to be a silver lining. Though I hadn't realized it at the time.

If I was with Maddox, I would never have a future with Galen. And I wanted that future. I wanted a happy ever after. With Galen.

I deserved that much.

So did Galen. I may have been inexperienced when it came to love, but I wasn't an idiot. Wolves don't throw a lot of mixed signals. The attraction is there, or it isn't. And it was definitely there with Galen.

The only thing that stood in our way was Galen's past and my present.

Old hang-ups and heartbreaks were tough to overcome, and I would have chalked that up to the biggest hurdle to our future together.

Until my eyes turned red.

I hoped the magic in the bracelet would hold because I needed to figure out what was wrong with me.

Or any chance at a future with Galen was over before it even began.

CHAPTER 10

GALEN

"This is incredible." Talia's eyes rounded into sapphire-violet saucers. "The amount of testosterone in the room is a bit overwhelming, but it's amazing how many packs there are. I had no idea."

"Yeah, it's amazing." I wished I shared her excitement.

The awe I'd felt attending my first summit had been replaced with been there, done that. Don't want to do it again.

The opening ceremony was the typical dog-and-pony show I'd come to expect from the council. Their grand entrance, complete with entourage, gave them a sense of importance and entitlement I wasn't sure they deserved.

It wasn't the council that was on the front lines against the demons and any other enemy out there. It was the packs.

Just like we were with everything else that came our way. The day-to-day life and survival of a pack had little to do with the council members who stood on that stage and demanded our allegiance.

Though some of the council members were pack Alphas, not all were. The pomp and ceremonies and oaths were just an attempt to keep the rest of us from figuring out which members were genuinely powerful, and which were full of crap.

Still, if there was ever a time to band together, and put my disdain for the council's political bullshit aside, it was now. While under a demon attack.

I couldn't sway the feeling that a war was coming, and if so, we needed every wolf to step up if we were to have any chance of stopping it.

"Alphas, your attention please." An ebony-skinned woman dressed to the nines in a sleek black form-fitting dress and red high heels took the stage.

Her voice boomed over the crowd without the assistance of a microphone. A rare female Alpha, she was used to speaking loud enough to be heard over a room full of stubborn men. The Alpha of a New Mexico territory, she was as vicious as any of her male counterparts and had earned her place on the council, not by appointment but through a challenge.

Which earned her the respect of every Alpha in attendance—including me.

"Take your places." She motioned to the center of the room and instructed the clusters of people forming alliances or negotiating challenges to put those conversations on hold until after the ceremony. "There will be time for that later. Right now, it is the council who requires your attention."

The first wave of power rippled through the room and Talia gasped. "What was that?"

It resonated out from the stage, like the soundwave from a tolling bell. But we felt these vibrations rather than hearing them.

"It's the pull of the council. Their bond supersedes any other pack bond." I enveloped her hand with mine and gave it a reassuring squeeze. "It's an equalizer. Or neutralizer, depending on how you look at it. Just take a deep breath. I know it feels weird, but it will pass."

"Weird is a bit of an understatement." Talia shivered, but she kept a firm grip on my hand. "Just how much control does the council have over the packs?"

"Here?" I asked for clarification and proceeded to answer at her nod. "On council land they have total control. It's not just in the Alpha bond, it's in the very land itself."

"In the land? But the bonds don't work that way." Talia's face scrunched up in obvious confusion. "Do they?"

"They do if they're magically enhanced, which they are, here. The magic is worked into the grounds by a local shaman and from what I'm told she is incredibly powerful."

"So, is it like total mind control?" Talia flicked her gaze to the council woman on the stage. Her brows furrowed, and her eyes narrowed. "They can just take away our free will if they want to?"

"No. Nothing like that," I reassured her. "They have a little more control over our wolves but not our human side. I'm not a fan of anything that overrides my pack bond, but there are a lot of Alphas and, as you pointed out, testosterone. The council needs to keep the peace."

"I guess." Talia sounded unconvinced.

Not that I blamed her.

The council, the rules and ceremonies, and the magical bond, were a lot to take in. I'd been skeptical my first time at the ranch. I probably still would have been, had Jarica, the Alpha from New Mexico, not assumed control of the council.

"The shaman, you said she's really powerful?" Talia rolled our entwined hands enough that I got a glimpse of the demon mark on her arm, but it remained hidden from everyone else. "I wish we had more time. It would be cool to meet her."

"I'll see what I can do."

Jarica raised her hand in the air and commanded the attention of everyone in the room. Silence fell over the crowd again as she stepped back up to the mic.

"Most if not all of you know why we gathered all of you here on such short notice." She pulled the microphone from its cradle on the metal stand and paced the stage, making direct eye contact with as many wolves as she could. "We are under attack right across the country, and so are the communities we call home."

"No kidding. What is the council going to do about it?" A man in a black and gray pinstriped suit with slicked back hair elbowed his way to the front of the crowd.

I couldn't place him or the pack he belonged to. I had no clue who he was or where he was from, but something told me Jarica knew and if she didn't, she would make it a point to find out.

"I would ask you the same question, sir." Jarica squatted down to eye level and held his gaze. "But before you answer, I will have your word."

The unknown Alpha tried and failed to disappear back into the crowd. But the wolves around him made sure to distance themselves, no doubt for fear they'd be associated with a troublemaker.

"The oath." Jarica stood to her full height and moved to center stage. "Each wolf here is bound to secrecy. What transpires here at the summit is for you and your packs. Some of you, the council included, have aligned themselves with a coven. You will not share the details of this summit with any witch without council approval."

The Alphas recited the oath, renewed their vow of secrecy and extended it to their packs. I spoke on behalf of Talia, Theo and every Long Claw member and agreed to bear the punishment should any of them violate the agreement.

An oath to the council wasn't something to be taken lightly. In fact, quite the opposite. Breaking the oath was punishable by death.

There was no death row and no appeals process. Just a one-way ticket to the executioner.

Since I planned on living a long and healthy life, it was up to me to ensure each member of my pack abided by the oath I'd sworn to uphold. The only surefire way to do that was through the pack bond.

I hated to force the will of the council on my wolves that way. It felt like a violation of their trust, but under the circumstances, I didn't have a choice.

"Now that we've gotten that formality out of the way, I believe the gentleman from the Arkansas pack had a question." Jarica strolled to the end of the stage and extended the mic, inviting the Alpha to take the floor.

He refused.

Smart man. I wouldn't have pressed my luck with Jarica either. She didn't get to her current position by being a docile wolf.

"If there's nothing further, the oath-taking ceremony is completed, and I hereby declare the first meeting of this summit adjourned. The western territories will report to the main conference room at three o'clock for debriefing on the demon attacks in their regions. We'll see the rest of you at the reception this evening."

Jarica attached the mic to the stand and exited the stage.

"There have to be over three hundred Alphas and Betas here." Talia watched with interest as the wolves filtered out of the meeting hall. "Is it always like this?"

Talia's awestruck expression reminded me of what it was like to see so many Alphas gathered in one room for the first time. I'd been just as overwhelmed when I'd attended my first summit.

The feeling faded with each meeting I'd attended over the years. Politics had a way of doing that.

"Yeah, it is." Theo squeezed through the crowd and joined us. "You'll get used to it."

"Where'd you come from?" Talia jumped at the sound of his voice and rounded on him, landing a light smack on his shoulder. "Don't do that."

"Oh, did I scare you?" Theo's smile ruined the effect of feigned remorse in his voice.

"I was distracted." Talia crossed her arms over her chest and jutted out one hip.

"What did you find out?" I nipped the sibling-like banter in the bud and redirected the conversation.

"There's two hundred and fifty Alphas registered at the ranch." Theo leaned in and lowered his voice. "And that includes the ones on the council."

"That means some of them refused to come." I did a rough estimate. Truth be told, I hadn't kept track of new packs that cropped up unless they were in or around my territory. "That's seventy-five, give or take a pack, that didn't bother showing up."

"Maybe the demon issue isn't as widespread as we thought, and they didn't see a point in coming?" Talia's ability to give the benefit of the doubt after everything her former pack had put her through amazed me.

"As much as I'd like to believe that's why they aren't here, I think the reasons are worse than ignorance of the situation. They're either making a break from the council and going rogue, or..." I couldn't bring myself to say it.

"Or what?" Talia asked, her eyes wide and worried. "What's worse than going rogue?"

"They're not here because they're dead," Theo said. The gravity of his answer was evident in the somber tone of his voice.

"Let's not jump to conclusions." I wanted to tamp down everyone's fears—mine included. "Theo, are you up for some more reconnaissance?"

"Some of the Betas put a poker game together. I'll check it out and see if I can steal more than just their money." Theo winked, said his goodbyes and went in search of the other Beta wolves.

"Come on, I'll take you back to the room." I wrapped my arm around Talia's waist, my fingers resting on her hip, and steered her toward the main doors.

"You don't really think the demons wiped out those packs?" She leaned in to whisper in my ear. "Do you?"

A passerby would have mistaken us for lovers, but our conversation couldn't have been further from sweet nothings or pillow talk.

"The truth?" I asked, not wanting to admit it to myself, let alone her.

If demons had overrun that many towns and taken out that many packs, things were worse than I thought.

"Of course, I want the truth."

I caught her wince and was reminded of our conversations before we'd left for the summit. There were still things she had yet to share with me.

"Then, yes. That is what I think."

We picked up our coats from the coat check, the UTV from the valet, and drove back to Harrier House.

"Hey, listen, I wasn't trying to upset you back there," I said into the silence. Her lack of response worried me. "You wanted me to be honest, but I didn't have to be blunt."

"No, it's not you—"

"Please don't follow that up with, it's me," I teased, and fished the room key out of my pocket to unlock the door.

"I was going to say it's the demons." Talia offered a genuine smile as she slipped past me and entered the efficiency.

"At the risk of sounding like a broken record, we are going to figure this out." I pushed the door closed with the sole of my shoe and crossed the room to join her on the loveseat.

"I know." She rubbed at the mark on her arm as if that would make the scar and our problems disappear.

"I mean it, Talia. I know with the Northwood pack and the demon attacks on the coven and in town it feels like you've been pushed to the back burner, but I haven't stopped searching for a way to remove the mark. It's all connected somehow. I won't stop until we have an answer."

I pinched her chin between my thumb and forefinger, turning her head until she was forced to look me in the eyes.

Her blue-violet eyes gleamed with unshed tears and my father's advice rang in my ears. She'd been through so much and had so many reasons not to trust anyone.

"I won't quit on you, Talia."

"I know." She closed her eyes, which forced the tears to spill over her lashes and track down her cheeks.

My heart ached for her pain. Jessie's death almost destroyed me, but my father and my friends had helped pick up the pieces of my shattered life and glue them back together. When Talia's world came crashing down around her, she'd had no one.

I wanted more than anything to help her, to be the glue that held her together. I wanted to be the man she needed. The man she wanted.

"Talia, you're safe with me. I want to take care of you, if you'll let me." I brushed the tears from her cheeks and cupped her face in my hands.

"I want that too, Galen." She leaned in, rested her forehead against mine and brushed our noses together.

Her lips were a hairsbreadth from mine. The slightest move and I could claim her mouth. My wolf stirred, encouraging me to claim her for our own.

As much as I wanted to take her right there on the couch, I needed her to make the first move. After her life had been ripped away from her, it was important that Talia take control of whatever happened between us.

It went against every Alpha instinct I had, but this had to be her choice.

I had to be her choice.

The attraction between us pulled both ways. I'd felt Talia's wolf respond to mine on more than one occasion, but she hadn't been ready to act on it before and I wouldn't force her to take things any further than she felt comfortable with.

If she wanted to take things slow, then that's what we'd do. Talia would set the pace.

She brought her hands to my face, cupped my jaw and pressed her lips to mine. She pulled my bottom lip into her mouth, nipping at it with her teeth.

A growl built in the back of my throat. My self-control hung by a thread. I ached to touch her, to explore every inch of her body until I knew every beauty mark or freckle by heart, but I dropped my hands to my sides.

What happened next had to be up to her.

"Galen." She took my hands and placed them on her hips, steadying herself as she climbed onto my lap and straddled me. "I want you to take care of me."

"Are you sure?" I rasped, my voice raw with need.

"I need this. Please." She kissed me again, deeper, rougher than the first time, and slid her hands under my shirt.

Her fingers explored my abs, trailed up my ribs and splayed across my chest. She sighed, slid her hands back down my sides, and gripped the hem of my shirt. I followed her lead and leaned forward. She pulled the t-shirt up and over my head and tossed it on the floor beside the loveseat.

I took my time undressing her, agonizing over each button on her blouse, before sliding it down her arms and dropping it on the floor beside mine. The soft pink lace pushup bra was the next to go.

My hands found their way up to her ample breasts. Her mewls of pleasure spurred me on. I rolled her pert nipples between my thumb and forefingers. She dropped her head backward and arched her back.

Once again, I followed her lead and unspoken commands, and pulled her breasts into my mouth, caressing first one and then the other of her nipples with my tongue.

I gripped her hips, pushing her down until her core pressed against the hard length of my erection trapped beneath my jeans.

"Galen." My name fell from her mouth like an erotic symphony. "Oh God, yes."

I shifted our position on the loveseat until she was on her back, unfastened the button on her jeans and inched them around the curve of her hips, down her legs and tugged her free of them.

Thumbs hooked on the narrow strips of lace on her matching panties, then they quickly joined the rest of her clothes in the pile on the floor.

Her breasts rose and fell with her ragged breathing as she fumbled with the button and zipper of my jeans. Talia slid her hand beneath the waistband of my boxer briefs and ran her hands along the hard length of my shaft.

She rolled her hips into my hand as I slid my fingers inside her. Her muscles clenched against my fingers as she rocked back and forth, heading closer to an orgasm.

"Not yet, baby," I whispered against her mouth. Coaxing her lips apart with my tongue, I poured everything she made me feel into the kiss. "Wait for me."

"Please, Galen. Hurry," she whimpered.

Her body trembling with need beneath me was enough to push me over the edge. I shoved my jeans and boxers down my hips and braced myself over her with my forearms against the side of the loveseat.

I rubbed the head of my dick against her clit before easing myself inside her. She sucked in a breath of air between her teeth and dug her nails into my hips.

"It stings a little." She slid her hands over my hips and gripped my ass, holding me in place.

Damn, in the heat of the moment I'd forgotten it was her first time.

Talia had just given herself and her virginity to me. It was the single sexiest experience I'd ever had with any woman, and it took everything I had not to orgasm right then.

"Are you okay?" I gritted my teeth and held as still as I could. "Do you want me to stop?"

She answered by raising her hips and pressing her core against me until I bottomed out inside her.

"Oh God, it hurts so good." She moaned and rocked her hips harder, faster, pushing me over the edge of my control. "Don't stop, Galen. Don't hold back."

I gripped her ass, fingers digging in as I lifted her up, adjusting the angle for deeper penetration. I matched her rhythm, pumping until she came.

"Galen." She screamed my name as the dam broke inside her and the first wave of her orgasm took her.

The pulse of her muscles when the second wave hit her tipped me over the edge into the longest, most intense orgasm I'd ever experienced. I hovered over her, as we both rode the last of the spasms and the sensitivity eased enough for me to pull out.

Out of breath, I collapsed on the couch cushion beside her. She turned to her side to spoon with her back pressed against my front. I wrapped my arm around her middle and pulled her tighter, until we were molded together.

My eyelids were heavy, but I refused to fall asleep. I was terrified I'd wake up and Talia would be gone.

I forced myself to stay awake, memorizing every detail in case our first time was our last.

CHAPTER 11

TALIA

A shrill ringing sound came from somewhere inside the pile of clothes on the floor.

"Ignore it." Galen held me tight against him.

The ringing stopped, only to start again a couple of seconds later.

"What if it's your dad or Theo?" I rolled onto my stomach, stretched over the side of the loveseat and rooted through the pile of hastily discarded clothes until I found his cell phone. "Three missed calls. All from Theo."

Galen offered his hand, pulled me back on the couch and nuzzled against me. He brushed my hair aside, exposed the sensitive skin on my neck and left a trail of fire in the wake of the kisses he planted from just beneath my ear down to my shoulder.

"Call him back," I said. "It must be important."

"This is important." His warm breath danced across my skin and sent shivers down my spine. "Part of me was afraid this was all a very vivid dream."

"I thought it was the woman who was supposed to get all emotional and clingy afterward," I teased, then rolled onto my left side to face him, pressed my lips to his and kissed him. "Call Theo back."

I untangled myself from his arms and legs, pushed off the couch and sorted the clothes on the floor, before heading to the bathroom to grab a hot shower.

Part of my pseudo-blasé attitude was to cover the residue of nerves I'd felt at having sex for the first time. I'd been so scared that I'd get it wrong, or Galen would suddenly decide he'd made a mistake, but that hadn't happened.

A huge grin split my face as I entered the bathroom and switched on the water.

My first time had been everything I'd hoped for and so much more.

Steam rolled out of the bathroom like a mystical fog when I emerged from the bathroom wrapped in thick, lush terrycloth towels. The beautiful and luxurious claw foot tub still called to me, beckoning me to submerge myself in hot, sudsy water to soak the sore muscles I hadn't known existed until after Galen and I had sex.

Galen had been generous and skilled when it came to love-making. Need pooled in my belly and the ache of desire built into a delicious pressure that I knew only Galen could satiate.

But the look on his face when I emerged from the bathroom said round two would have to wait.

"What did Theo say?" I adjusted the towel wrapped around my body and sat next to him on the edge of the couch.

"The council moved up the debriefing time and changed it to Alphas only. I have just enough time to get cleaned up and then I have to go." He leaned in and pressed a kiss to my cheek. "Did you save any hot water for me?"

"Probably not, but I think you'd benefit more from a cold shower anyway."

I gave him a playful nudge and sent him on his way to take a shower while I slipped into a pair of yoga pants, matching tank top and my favorite pair of argyle slipper socks.

The council's decision to change the debriefings to a closed-door meeting provided some unexpected me-time that I wasn't about to let go to waste.

My wolf's restlessness had been sated in some ways, but not in others. She needed to stretch her legs, run, wild and free outside without worry that Galen would see our eyes.

Of course, I still ran the risk of being caught by someone else.

The last thing I needed was an Alpha from a neighboring territory to learn of my condition before Galen did. Or worse, using it as blackmail for leverage in a future pack negotiation.

Which meant I had to be careful.

And the same rules applied at the ranch as at home. My wolf skulked into the shadows of my mind, disappointed to be reined in yet again. I felt the same way. I wanted to feel the grass beneath our paws, the cool air ruffling through my coat and run until I collapsed from exhaustion.

It's good to want things. It builds character.

My father used to tell me that when I was a little girl and I never understood what it meant. But I was starting to.

"Whoa." Galen shouted from inside the bathroom.

The water shut off and the metal shower curtain rings skated along the metal pole above the shower.

"Everything okay?" I called out, hopping off the couch and skipping across the hardwood floor to the bathroom.

"We're officially out of hot water." Galen wrapped a towel around his waist and used another to dry his hair.

No one had a right to be that perfect. I didn't even bother to hide the fact that I was checking him out while he got dressed.

"I don't think I've ever had a woman look at me like that while I put my clothes on." Galen laughed, buttoned his jeans and pulled the fitted navy-blue tee shirt over his head.

The fabric had to be listed among the seven wonders of the modern world from the way it stretched over well-defined pectorals, chiseled abs and muscular arms.

"Sorry." I covered my mouth with my hands, hiding my mischievous smile from view.

"I don't think you are, and I don't want you to be." Galen pulled my hands down from my face and planted a kiss on my lips.

The cool mint of his toothpaste mixed with the earthy scent of his cologne. It was a heady combination and a surprising turn-on.

"You better get a move on or you're going to be late." I nipped his bottom lip.

"I have time." He deepened the kiss until I pulled back and untangled myself from his embrace.

"Not that kind of time, mister." I grabbed a hand towel, twirled it into a rope and snapped it against his backside. "Go to your meeting. The sooner you get done the sooner you get back."

He grabbed his coat, the key for the UTV and rushed out the door with promises to pick up where we left off when he returned.

At least I had one thing to look forward to.

As much as I wanted and needed to run, a part of me did not look forward to taking off the bracelet Sarah gave me and shifting into my wolf form.

My wolf deemed me a chicken and proceeded to discuss how delicious poultry was. Meanwhile, I made a mental note to hit the snack basket the ranch stocked our room with after I came back from my run.

Pretzels and peanuts weren't the wild game she needed, but they would have to do. We couldn't risk a hunt. Not until we knew the grounds and where the other wolves hunted.

I slipped the bangle off my wrist, undressed and called my wolf.

The magic inherent in all shifters that controlled our dual

nature rippled through my body. Fur replaced skin, bones shifted, claws replaced nails, teeth shifted and elongated.

And my eyes turned red.

I caught a glimpse of my reflection in the window and padded into the bathroom, propping my front paws up on the counter in order to get a better look in the mirror.

They were worse.

The red, more pronounced than it had been before we left for the summit, had overtaken the whites of my eyes. It looked as if multiple blood vessels had burst and I was hemorrhaging in my eyes.

If I had been any other creature than a shifter, that might have worked as a cover for whatever was really going on with my eyes. But wolves healed. The blood vessels would repair themselves and the blood would be absorbed back into my body.

Our regenerative abilities made calling in sick for work difficult to say the least.

I'd only ever known one wolf who hadn't been able to heal himself and that was Max. Faking another case of Max's mystery disease would have worked if our symptoms were similar. They weren't.

Illness and injury were still out.

Which left me with no alternative but to stay the course. Avoid spending any amount of time with Galen in my wolf form and wearing my enchanted bracelet at all times in my human form.

I snuck out of the cabin, hyper aware of my surroundings and in touch with my senses. When I had thoroughly scented the air and was sure there were no other wolves in the close proximity, I gave my wolf a small taste of freedom.

She caught sight of a sharp-tailed grouse and pounced, flushing the bird from the brush that camouflaged it from most predators. The bird flapped its wings and took flight. My wolf gnashed her teeth and leapt after it, snapping her jaws mid-air.

She landed on all four paws, defeated, with only two tail feathers instead of a whole bird in her mouth.

Something larger than a wolf approached from the east. The gravel crunched beneath their feet as they made their way up the path that led to the Harrier House cabin. I counted two footsteps, not four. Whoever approached was in human form.

I was upwind and unable to catch a scent, but I knew it wasn't Galen. The cadence of the person's walk was different. They were heavy footed, and a man if I had to guess.

Theo?

It didn't matter who it was. I needed to get back inside and transform into my human self before they caught sight of a red-eyed wolf lurking on the property.

Somehow, I managed to scramble fast and made it back inside just before the visitor mounted the porch. "Talia, you home?" It was Theo. He knocked on the door before he let himself in.

"Just a sec. I'm in the bathroom." I'd made it into the small ensuite, grabbed a mouthful of clothes and shifted back with seconds to spare.

"Take your time. Galen asked me to drop in and check on you." He was rooting through the snack basket when I stepped out of the bathroom. "You guys have jerky and mini chocolate chip cookies in yours? I'll trade you two bags of trail mix for one bag of jerky."

"Are there candy-coated chocolate pieces in the trail mix?" When he shook his head no, I upped the ante. "Three bags or no deal."

"You drive a hard bargain."

"True." I shrugged. "You want the jerky or not?"

"Obviously." Theo pointed to a stack of garment bags laying on the mattress. "Galen asked me to drop those off for you."

He bolted out the door to the loft efficiency on the second floor and zipped back a couple of minutes later with the bags of trail mix, ready to make a trade.

"Galen has excellent taste." I laid the dresses out on the bed. "Are these for the gala?"

"These are for dinner tonight." Theo offered a meager smile. "Apparently, it's semi formal wear. Which I think means I need to wear a tie?"

"Suit and tie, but not a tux." I stared at the variety of cocktail dresses ranging from vintage black velvet with a v-neck and petticoat to the classic Hepburn little black dress complete with pearl choker.

"Which one do you like the best?" They were all gorgeous and I couldn't make up my mind.

"I can barely pick out my own clothes, and you want me to pick out your dress? I like the black one." Theo made a broad sweeping gesture to all of the dresses I'd laid out on the bed.

"They're all black." I turned and leveled him with my best glare.

"I'm going to go watch an online tutorial on how to tie a tie." Theo made a dash for the door, and a hasty retreat to the loft, and left me to decide for myself.

I glanced at the cuckoo clock mounted on the wall above a small side table by the door.

"I'll just have to try them all," I muttered to myself, slipping the first dress off the hanger.

By the time Galen came to collect me for dinner, I'd held my own haute couture runway show and left a trail of black cocktail dresses in my wake.

"Wow." Galen raked his gaze over my body, leaving my skin scorched and the rest of me aching with need. "You look amazing. That dress is wow."

"You said that already," I teased, with a sultry smile on my face, and adjusted the off-shoulder sleeve of my dress.

"The fact that my adjectives are limited to one, should tell you how amazing you look."

"That's two adjectives." I raised my arms at my sides and did a slow three-sixty for the full view at his request.

I'd chosen the eyelash crochet black lace with nude underlay, plunging neckline and perilously high slit.

He licked his lips, rolling his bottom lip between his teeth as he continued to ogle every curve on display in the form-fitting dress.

"If you keep looking at me like that, we'll never make it to the welcome dinner." Heat flushed my cheeks and pooled between my legs.

"Sorry, my mind is already on dessert." Galen took my hand in his and pulled me against him, nuzzling into my neck with tender kisses.

I imagined the things he wanted to do to me and all but melted in his arms.

"Well then, I guess it's a good thing we're already dressed, and Theo is on his way downstairs." I tilted my head to one side and eyed the ceiling. "Or our table would be missing two guests."

Galen looked good enough to eat, dressed in a black on black, custom fitted suit. I couldn't wait to watch him take it off. Clearly, it only took one time with Galen to turn me into a fiend.

Theo's heavy footfalls crossed the room above us and the front door of his efficiency thumped closed behind him.

"Anticipation heightens the experience." Galen's wicked smile tipped my hormones over the edge and left me counting the minutes until we were alone again.

"You two decent?" Theo called out from the other side of our door and rapped his knuckles on the center glass windowpane.

"I've got the plastic cab zipped onto the UTV and she's all warmed up."

The UTV wasn't the only thing that was warmed up. If I could have come up with a way for us to skip the reception, I would have. Something told me Galen wouldn't have needed much convincing.

"Come on, let's go." I laced my fingers with his and tugged him toward the door. "Like you said, anticipation—"

"Heightens the experience. I know what I said." Galen shook his head and let out a delicious, husky laugh. "I just can't stop thinking about the experience part."

The dress provided a wonderful distraction for me and Galen, but it did nothing against the cold. Neither did the flimsy plastic sheeting attached to the UTV. Galen took off his suit jacket and draped it over my shoulders, but my teeth chattered the whole way to the banquet room.

We reached the ranch's main building, weaved our way through the crowd lingering in the lobby and found our way to our assigned seats. Galen pulled out the middle chair and sat me between him and Theo.

"Is there something I should be worried about?" I smoothed the backside of my dress and sat down as Galen scooted me in closer to the table.

The seating arrangement felt intentional, and I couldn't help but wonder if he knew something about my safety that I didn't. Had someone heard about my demon mark?

At least it was the mark and not demon eyes. No one knew about that development, but Sarah, and she was miles away.

"Nothing we can't handle." Galen and Theo glared at the guests seated at a table three over on the right of ours.

Maddox and his father.

I should have known they would be here. The Northwood pack attended every summit. I'd secretly hoped after the losses they suffered when they attacked the Long Claw pack, they would have skipped this one.

To my relief, dinner was delicious and uneventful. Each course was a new culinary treat selected from the regions of each of the packs in attendance. The conversation was focused on politics, the demon attacks, and more politics.

My name never came up once, apart from introductions as other guests seated themselves at our table.

Even Maddox and his father behaved themselves; never once approaching our table. The night would have been flawless, if not for one guest who couldn't seem to take her eyes off me.

The woman hadn't bothered to hide her interest. When I'd caught her staring at me on more than one occasion, she didn't so much as blink or look away. Had we met before? It seemed unlikely. She would presumably have stopped at our table and struck up a conversation or tried to jog my memory.

She did neither.

A chill ran down my spine, raising the hairs on the back of my neck and arms. Something bad was about to happen. I could sense it.

I didn't know what or where, but the one thing I did know was it had everything to do with her.

CHAPTER 12

GALEN

"Are you having a good time?" I draped my arm over Talia's shoulder and tucked her into my side.

"I am. Dinner was lovely." She nestled into the crook of my neck and sighed. "I'm stuffed and testing the limits of this dress. If I eat another bite, I think I'll bust a seam."

She sounded genuine, content, but I'd spent enough time around Talia to know when something was bothering her.

And something—or someone—definitely was.

"They're not going to start anything. If they were, they would have done it before dinner started. Not at the end." I made the logical assumption it was her ex-fiancé and his Alpha-hole father.

"I didn't realize there was a protocol to follow for picking a fight." Talia laughed but her usual singsong cadence was gone.

"Hey, look at me." I adjusted our seating until she could meet my gaze. "They are not going to bother you tonight. Or any other night. I promise."

"That's sweet." She pressed a kiss to my lips, nipping my bottom lip with her incisor. "But you shouldn't make promises you can't keep."

"He doesn't." Theo pushed his cake plate toward the center of the table, removed the napkin from his lap and set it on the table.

When Maddox and his father said their goodbyes and left the banquet room, Theo fell in step behind them.

"Where's he going?" Talia tracked Theo as he left the reception, but quickly returned her attention back to the guests.

One in particular, and the woman hadn't been seated at the same table as the Northwood pack.

"To get our coats." I followed her line of sight to an elderly woman a few tables over.

So, who was she and how did Talia know her?

"We didn't check any coats." Talia spared a glance at the exit. "Is he following Maddox?"

I evaded her question with one of my own.

"An old friend of yours?" I asked, curious to know if the older woman had been a Northwood pack member at one time and been banished like Talia. "Maybe someone you recognize from your old pack?"

"No." Talia's answer was as clipped as her tone.

"So, why are we staring at her?" I couldn't help feeling as if I'd missed something important while I'd been engrossed in a meaningless conversation about national politics.

I had zero interest in a position on the council. My pack was, is and always would be enough for me. My aspirations for leadership stopped there.

While I'd been distracted by a wolf from Arizona seated on my right, Talia had some sort of interaction with a strange old woman across the room.

"Because she started staring at me first." Talia shook her head and laughed under her breath. "It sounds ludicrous and juvenile now that I've said it out loud."

"Maybe a little." I teased and gave her side a playful pinch.

"But, you know, maybe not. I'll ask around. See if I can find out who she is."

"I'm probably overreacting. Maybe she's just staring off in a daze and isn't even staring at me at all."

"It's possible. Let's test that theory." I pushed my chair back from the table and stood, easing Talia's chair back from the table and helping her to her feet.

I rested my hand on the small of her back and escorted her out of the banquet room and into the lobby.

"She tracked you as you walked out of the room." I caught sight of Theo and called him over. "I'm not sure why you caught her interest, but I'm going to find out."

"I'm sure it's nothing. Let's not make a big deal about it. At least not yet." Talia reached for the thin black satin wrap in Theo's hands and draped it over her shoulders. "You need to stay focused on why we're here. The demons."

"Who do I need to follow now?" Theo scanned the room. "I thought this was going to be a mini vacation. If I'd have known how much work this was going to be, I wouldn't have volunteered."

"Don't act like you're not having the time of your life. You love recon." I clapped him on his shoulder and pointed him in the direction of his new target.

"The harmless old lady?" Theo scoffed, shrugging off my suspicions. "She looks like someone's sweet old granny. How much do you want to bet she has tissues and butterscotch candies in her purse?"

"There isn't a harmless person on this ranch, and you know it." I crooked my elbow and, as I'd hoped, Talia hooked her arm through mine.

I'd brought her with me to keep her safe. I never expected our relationship to progress so quickly, but I was glad it had. So was my wolf. He'd wanted to claim her the first moment we laid eyes on her.

"Point taken." Theo narrowed his gaze, scrutinizing the old crone. "Still, out of all the wolves here, I think she's the least of our problems. Maybe she's just a nosy old lady."

"That's what you're going to find out." I gave him his orders and sent him off to gather as much information as he could on the woman.

What territory and pack she belonged to, her rank, and if she had any connections to Northwood. I wanted to know every detail.

"Excuse me." A man I recognized from the briefing, but whose name escaped me, walked over and extended his hand. "It's Galen, right? From the Long Claw pack?"

"It is." I clasped his hand in a firm grip and gave him a hearty shake. "I'm sorry, I know we met earlier, but I'm terrible with names."

"Victor. Victor Curry, from the Mount Bona pack."

"Right, right. Sorry about that, Victor." I released his hand from mine, crossed my arms over my chest and took two steps to my right, positioning myself between him and Talia. "What can I do for you?"

If Victor found my cut to the chase approach to our conversation rude, he didn't show it.

"I was impressed with your detailed briefing this afternoon." He cocked his head to one side, brows furrowed, and looked over my shoulder at Talia.

"Thanks." I sidestepped once more, blocking Talia from his view. "Listen, we were just leaving. It was nice meeting you, Victor. Let's catch up after the next debriefing, all right?"

"Forgive me, but I feel like we've met before." Victor pointed over my shoulder, indicating that he was talking to Talia. Then his glance returned to me. "The beautiful young lady behind you, she reminds me of someone I met years ago, and I—"

"We've never met, I assure you. I'm Talia Linetti." She stepped out from behind me, stood at my side and hooked her arm through mine. "I think I would remember meeting a wolf from somewhere as far away as Alaska. The ranch is the furthest I've ever been from home."

"I would hope I'd leave an impression strong enough to be remembered as well. My mistake."

He clasped his hands together in front of his chest and dipped his head in a gesture of apology, before turning his attention to a conversation about demons.

"You've had more experience with demons than any other Alpha here," he said. "I mean, there have been more attacks in your territory than anywhere else. I find that interesting and can't help but wonder if there is some reason for it. Why do you think there are so many attacking your region?"

I'd been asked the same questions during the debriefing and assumed Victor had been present to hear my answers. Did he expect something different from me in a one-on-one situation? His fishing expedition was about to come to an end, because I wasn't biting.

Talia and I had after-dinner plans.

"Not all of the Alphas have made their presentations. Other regions may be experiencing concentrated attacks as well." I dipped my chin and looked at Talia. "You ready?"

She nodded and I took a step to the right, steering us around Victor and closer to the door, but the wolf from the northwest was as relentless as an Alaskan winter.

"TRUE, but you've been forced to move an entire coven of witches onto your property. It's unprecedented and makes for quite a powerful alliance, wouldn't you say?"

Victor's not-so-subtle approach about the strength of my pack only served to test my patience.

"First of all, I wasn't forced to do anything. We've had an

alliance with our local coven for years. The Longclaw pack protects what's theirs." I clapped my hand on his shoulder. "It was nice talking with you, Victor, but as you can imagine, this beautiful woman and I have other plans."

"Yes, of course. I didn't mean to intrude on your evening." Victor put his hands behind his back and gave a slight bow. "Another time."

He slipped back into the crowd, mingling with the other Alphas as we made our way out the door to the valet station where our UTV was waiting for us.

"You're a popular girl." I unzipped the makeshift door of plastic sheeting on the passenger side of the UTV and helped Talia into the seat.

"It's weird, right?" She waited to finish her thought until I came around to the driver's side and had us sealed as tight as we would be in the temporary cover. "I mean, first that old woman stared at me all through dinner and now this guy, Victor? I've never seen him before. I remind him of a woman he used to know? I wonder who she is."

"Yeah, that would be one hell of a coincidence and I don't really believe in coincidences. Hopefully, Theo will have some information about the old woman in a few hours."

"I hope so too." Talia wrung her hands together in her lap. "I'm sorry for causing more trouble. It really does seem to follow me wherever I go."

"On the upside, no one could ever accuse you of being boring." I turned the key, pulled away from the ranch's meeting hall, and drove us back to our cabin.

"I used to be." Talia stifled a bitter laugh and ticked off a litany of reasons. "Waited tables, abstinent, monogamous relationship, same friends since childhood, never strayed further than neutral ground or my pack's land. The old me was pretty damn boring. You wouldn't have given her a second look or thought."

"Trust me Talia, I had far more than a second thought the day I saw you in town. There were a million thoughts running through my mind and not one of them was boring."

I liked the fact that I could make her cheeks pinken up. I shot a grin at her as I parked the UTV in front of the cabin, hopped out and rushed around to the passenger side to unzip the door and help her out.

"Took you long enough." Theo was in our cabin. He rummaged through the mini bar and poured three small bottles into glasses filled with ice. "Whiskey, tequila, or rum? Pick your poison."

"Hi, Theo." Talia strolled into the cabin seemingly unphased by my Beta's unexpected presence. "A man named Victor from Alaska stopped us on our way out. He was interested in the demon attacks. Among other things."

She dropped her clutch purse and satin wrap onto the armchair and chose a random glass from the console table behind the loveseat.

"What other things?" Theo arched a quizzical brow and tossed the empty bottles into the trash can. "Was he asking about you, Talia?"

"Shouldn't you be at a bingo game or playing canasta or something?" I grumbled, snatching the glass of whiskey Theo had chosen for himself. Talia had nabbed the rum and there was no way I was knocking back tequila. "I thought I told you to follow the old woman, see what you could find out about her?"

I'd had enough distractions for one evening. All I wanted to do was spend time alone with Talia. I'd promised her dessert and I intended to deliver.

"I did." Theo eyed the remaining tequila with disappointment, shivering when he slammed it back, and then poured himself another from a different small bottle. "Or at least, I tried to. She gave me the slip."

"What?" Talia and I asked almost in unison.

"How?" I added. "No one can clock you when you don't want to be seen."

"I don't know how she did it, Galen. I was on the trail. I had her scent. There were tracks. I mean, I was practically right on top of her and then... nothing. Clean air, clean snow. It's like she vanished into thin air."

"Damn." I held up my hand, stopping Theo's next defensive argument before it started.

He didn't need to explain himself to me. If I didn't think he was capable of tracking a wolf in her twilight years, I wouldn't have asked him to do it. I had every confidence in my Betas. All three of them.

They wouldn't be in the position otherwise.

"So, what do we do now?" Ice cubes clinked against the side of Talia's glass as she nursed her drink.

Meanwhile I ransacked the mini bar for two more nips of whiskey.

"There isn't anything else we can do. At least not tonight." I took a long pull from my glass, savoring the smoky flavor and slow burn of the alcohol.

"Actually, there is something." Theo sat up, sloshing ice and liquid over the rim of his glass.

"And that something would be?" I asked, while I took quick stock of the remaining mini bottles of liquor.

It took a lot to get a shifter drunk and it seemed obvious he'd helped himself to the alcohol before we arrived. Whether he'd simply had a few, or a few too many, was yet to be determined.

"Wait, you said a guy from Alaska?" Theo set his glass on the table and tipped the scales toward a few too many with his abrupt change of subject.

"Yeah, Victor. What of him?" I tugged at my tie, loosening the knot around my neck before undoing the top button at the collar of my shirt.

My night with Talia had not gone according to plan and seemed to be offering up yet another detour.

"I think he might be there."

"Where? Theo, you're not making a whole lot of sense right now." Talia finished her drink and set the empty glass beside the metal ice bucket.

"Sorry, I was just thinking how weird it is that two people were focused more on Talia tonight than the Long Claw Alpha." He turned to Talia. "No offense. I mean, you're attention-worthy. It's just... Alpha usually trumps everything else."

"I know. No offense taken." Talia shook her head, a lopsided smile planted on her face.

"Probably not a coincidence. We came to the same conclusion." I took my frustration out on the black satin tie, yanked it free of my neck and tossed it on the chair with Talia's things. "Where is it exactly that you think this Victor guy might be?"

"There's a midnight run. A lot of the people were talking about it during the poker game." Theo pulled a trifold brochure itinerary from his inner jacket pocket and tapped it against his palm. "Any takers?"

I hadn't heard anything about poker or group hunts. All of my conversations had involved politics and demons. It was a good thing the council authorized two companions for the summit. Otherwise, my time would have been too divided and Talia would have had to snoop on her own.

And there was no way in hell that was going to happen.

"What do you say, Talia?" I slipped off my suit jacket and unbuttoned the cuffs on my sleeves. "You up for a run and some reconnaissance?"

She hesitated, before pointing to the old fashioned clawfoot soaker by the window. "The only thing I'm up for is a soak in that tub." She sighed loudly. "I've had my fill of strangers for the night. Is it all right with you if I sit this one out?"

"Of course." My gaze lingered on the soaker tub. My imagination ran wild, and I found myself wanting to skip the run as well.

For more than one reason.

I hated to leave her alone. Harrier House was the furthest cabin from the main building. If something happened, there was a real possibility help might not reach her in time.

Still, I'd seen her fight. I knew Talia could handle herself against another wolf—and even a demon. I would make sure I only ran for a short time and didn't leave her alone too long.

Still, I also knew that if something happened to her, I would never forgive myself.

· CHAPTER 13

TALIA

The cabin was empty, and the soaker tub was full. I hadn't lied to Galen about the tub. I'd thought about sinking up to my neck in hot sudsy water since we arrived. If only Galen had been here to enjoy it with me.

There wasn't any room for anger or disappointment over the way our night had turned out. It wasn't Galen's fault he had to leave. If anyone was to blame, it was me.

I could leave my pack, my town, and even the state. It didn't matter where I went. Trouble always found me.

And Galen had been there to patch me up and clean up the mess.

If I hadn't been riddled with guilt over not telling him the truth about my wolf's eyes before I slept with him, I sure as hell was now.

Why wasn't I able to tell him? I wished I knew the answer to that question. My life and our relationship would have been so much simpler if I'd told him from the start.

Instead, I had managed to complicate everything and build our relationship on a lie.

I contemplated my life and possible future with Galen until the bubbles disappeared and the water turned cold. Water dripped off my legs and soaked into the buttercream-colored bath rug as I stepped over the tub's edge.

The cabin door jostled.

"Galen, is that you?" Two terrycloth towels in hand, I wrapped one around my body and twisted the other around my hair. "Did you forget your key?"

I crossed the cabin's hardwood floor as fast as I could with wet feet and opened the door.

"Miss me?" Maddox leered from the other side of the doorway.

"Not even a little bit." I moved to slam the door in his face, but his size fourteen black biker boot blocked it from closing. "Get your foot out of the door."

"Come on, Talia." Maddox reached through the ten-inch gap and brushed his fingers along my forearm. "You don't expect me to believe that you don't want to see me, do you? When I saw you tonight at dinner, I realized I missed you."

He had me at a disadvantage. I wasn't dressed for company—or a fight.

Not to mention the fact that I couldn't use my body weight to hold the door and escape his reach. I had no intention of letting him inside the cabin. Which meant I needed to stay put and Maddox was free to touch any part of my body within reach.

"After all the years we were together? Not even a teensy-weensy bit? I was your first boyfriend, your first kiss, your first everything." He moved from my arm to my leg, inching his hand further up my left thigh until he reached the edge of the towel.

"You weren't my first for everything, Maddox," I snapped back without a thought as to how he might react.

That was a mistake.

"You slept with him?" Maddox fisted his hand in the towel and tugged. "You certainly didn't waste any time giving up the goods to a total stranger."

My knee-jerk reaction was to grab the towel and put as much distance between me and Maddox as possible.

Which was exactly what he wanted. He pushed the door wider and stepped in.

"You sure put me through the ringer, didn't you? Promise rings and all that bullshit about waiting for our wedding night." His voice dropped an octave and his pupils dilated. His wolf was close to the surface.

Tread carefully, Talia. Don't be stupid. There would come a day when I would take my own advice, but today wasn't it.

"I thought you wanted to wait too. You said—"

"Yeah, that's what every guy wants. To wait." A low growl rumbled up from the depths of his chest. "Because that's how you ended up on your back for your new boyfriend, right? Waiting?"

"Get out." I pointed to the open door, oblivious to the frigid air that poured in. The banked rage I felt kept me plenty warm. "Now."

"I should have listened to my father. He always said you were a whore. Just like your mother." Maddox sneered, revealing elongated incisors.

The better to eat you with, my dear.

"You're a cold-hearted bastard. Just like your father. I was an idiot for loving you." I held my ground and motioned toward the door again. "Get. Out."

"If this wasn't a peaceful summit, I would drop you where you stand." Maddox stalked toward me, closing the distance between us and forcing me further inside the cabin with no way out but past him. "Traitorous bitches like you deserve to be put down."

"Traitorous? You threw me out, remember?" I'd anguished for weeks, stewed in the pain of his rejection and betrayal, and all the pent-up emotions suddenly boiled over. I screamed at the top of my lungs.

"Get the fuck out of my cabin, you crazy bastard!"

But Maddox had me right where he wanted me. Alone.

"Looks like someone's forgotten their place." Maddox lunged forward, grabbed me by the arms and yanked me hard enough to snap my head forward and smack my teeth together. "New boyfriend, new pack, new attitude, is that it? You may have them fooled, but I know better. This isn't you."

"You don't know me at all." I jerked my arms, fighting to free myself from his grip to no avail.

"No?" He leaned in, close enough that our noses touched. "I know you well enough to know that you're hiding something."

"You lost any claim you had over my secrets when you broke off the engagement."

"As if you could actually keep a secret from me." He barked out an angry, bitter laugh. "Nobody knows you like I do, Talia. I know you better than anybody."

"Why do you suppose that is?"

I didn't bother waiting for a response. The question had been rhetorical.

"It couldn't possibly have anything to do with the fact that your father killed the only family I had left, could it?"

That had been rhetorical too, but Maddox answered anyway. He couldn't help himself. He never had been the brightest bulb on the tree. Of course, the same argument could have been made for me since I'd fallen for him.

At least I had naivety as an excuse.

"Your father was nothing but a screw up. An old dog with no new tricks. If you ask me, it was a mercy killing. You should be thanking my father instead of blaming him."

He tightened his grip, ratcheting his fingers around my arms hard enough to leave bruises. I wouldn't be able to hide those without shifting, and even then, the discoloration wouldn't disappear completely.

Galen would know Maddox had been here, even without the marks on my skin. His scent permeated the efficiency. If the Northwood and Long Claw packs weren't already at war, they soon would be.

It was time for Maddox to get the hell out of the cabin and out of my life. For good.

"You're hiding something, Talia Linetti. I'm going to find out what it is." Maddox wedged his face between my jaw and shoulder and breathed me in like a predator does their prey when they are about to strike the killing blow.

I stomped my foot as hard as I could on top of his, but the boot's protective steel toe blunted the impact. Maddox leaned backward and laughed in my face. He gave me a clean shot and I wasn't about to waste it. I reared back and smashed my forehead against his nose.

It broke with a satisfying crunch and a trickle of blood.

"You bitch. You just broke my nose."

Maddox let go of my left arm, pulled back and landed an open hand smack to the left side of my face from the corner of my eye to the corner of my mouth. I licked the blood from my split lip and cheek and spat on the toe of his boot.

"This whole pack princess dream of yours will come crashing down around you. Galen won't want you; I sure as hell don't want you."

Without warning, Maddox grabbed a fist full of my damp hair, yanked my head to one side and bit down. His teeth pierced through my skin and gouged into my collar bone.

In the space of a split second, Maddox marked me.

The claim he staked by notching my clavicle wasn't the same as a fated mate bond. There wouldn't be a ring or a ceremony. The only vow Maddox made by marking me was to never let me go. That mark meant I was his property. He owned me.

Or at least, he thought he did.

It was yet another claim on my body, on my life, from someone or something I didn't want, and I would be damned if I would let him get away with it. A sob-turned-scream tore its way out of my body. Fueled by rage, my nails shifted into claws. I slashed him across his face.

The marks on his face and his broken nose would heal, unlike the mark on my collar bone, but it still felt good. I'd drawn blood and his father would see it. The Northwood pack would see it.

"Your boyfriend should be home any minute. I want to leave a good impression." Maddox punched me in the solar plexus, knocking the wind out of me and dropping me to my knees. He ripped the towel that hung loose around my body and tossed it far out of arm's reach.

He left me there sprawled on the floor, naked and gasping for air.

I sucked in a breath, only to cough and expel it all out again. The warmth from the underlay heating system seeping up through the floorboards was useless against the bitter cold of a Montana night that rolled into the cabin through the open door.

My temper had dissipated once Maddox left. Now my teeth chattered, the frigid air stung my skin and lungs, and I developed the shakes as my body tried to generate more body heat. I needed to move or die of exposure on the cabin floor.

I had two choices.

Option A. Find the will to pick myself up off the floor and carry my naked self to the door, close it and build a fire. Practical and possible, despite the humiliation that kept me planted to the floor.

Option B. Shift. Allow my wolf to heal those injuries she could and provide the warmth we needed with a form better suited to survive the cold than a human's.

It was damned if you do, damned if you don't.

Either option would raise questions. Questions that I wasn't ready to answer—because I didn't have an answer.

If I didn't shift, Galen would want to know why. There would be questions about my wolf. Had Maddox done something to injure her and prevent me from shifting? And if I did shift? Well, he would see my eyes, the truth would be exposed, and everything would be ruined.

A third option struck while I staggered upright and stacked logs inside the cast iron stove.

There were enough hot coals left on the grate to catch the seasoned split wood and start a crackling fire. I hurried to lock the door, rushed back to the heat billowing out of the pot-bellied wood stove and knelt on the warm inlay stone flooring beneath it.

I closed my eyes and called to my wolf. She howled her reply. The magic that controlled our shift vibrated through my bones like a tuning fork, searching for the right pitch and frequency to create the change.

Bones cracked, dislocated and rearranged themselves. My jaw unhinged and elongated with my teeth. My hair grew longer, coarser and filled in to create a thick, lush midnight-black coat unlike any wolf I'd ever known.

I curled up on the stone floor in front of the wood stove and tucked my head beneath my front paws with my eyes shut tight.

Galen kicked open the front door and charged in with Theo right behind him.

"Talia." He rushed over and knelt beside me, burying his fingers in my fur. "Are you hurt? What did he do to you? I'll kill him."

I didn't need to open my eyes to know that Galen's wolf was

close to the surface. Theo's, too. I felt them through the pack bond, and I heard it in their voices as they tried to examine me for injuries.

My wolf knew the plan and for once agreed to play along. It seemed like ages since we'd agreed on anything, but even she knew it was dangerous for anyone to see her red eyes. She relinquished power over my body and stalked back into the shadows of my soul where she lurked until I, or the pull of the moon, called her.

The physical changes happened in reverse and my human form reappeared, curled in the fetal position on the floor next to Galen.

"Theo, grab a blanket." His voice was gravelly and raw from the strain of holding back his own change.

Nothing sent an Alpha into overdrive like an injured pack member.

"I'll get her some water." Theo draped a quilt over my body. "And then I'll make her some tea. It's like a sauna in here and she's still shivering."

"It's not because she's cold." Galen bundled me in the quilt, scooped me onto his lap and pushed stray hairs away from my face.

"Tea sounds good." I molded my body to Galen's, absorbing his body heat and relishing the comfort the woodsy-citrus scent of his cologne brought me. "Actually, hot chocolate sounds better."

"Hot chocolate coming up." Theo seemed all too happy to distract himself and his wolf rustling through canisters and cabinets for instant cocoa powder and a pot to prepare it in.

"Talia, I don't mean to push you too soon, but can you please tell me what happened?" Galen stroked my hair, the side of my face and along my neck.

His fingers stilled when they brushed against my collar bone and found the notch in my clavicle.

Galen went glacial. "I am going to kill him." It was my first real glimpse of the true predator he shared his soul with. "And then I'm going to kill his father."

"Galen." I pressed my hand against his jaw and brushed my thumb along his cheek bone. "That's what he wants. He wants you to declare war in the middle of the summit."

"Yeah? Well, if it's war he wants, then it's war he'll get." I felt the growl that rumbled through his chest. "I would say he'll live to regret this, but that would be a lie."

"Galen, listen to her." Theo set a cast iron pot filled with water to boil on the wood stove. "She's right. He's baiting the hook. Don't do this. Not here."

"Maddox started this and I'm going to finish it." Galen clutched me to his chest, holding me tighter than he ever had. "I'll talk to the council. They'll understand."

"Will they?" I asked, hoping he would listen to reason.

"I'll make them."

"No, you won't." I cupped his face in both hands and pulled his head down, forcing him to meet my gaze. "Every wolf here took the same oath. Peace during the summit. All other pack affairs are to be put aside. The only thing the council wants brought before it is business dealing with the demons."

"If they knew what he did to you, that he marked you as his property—"

"I won't tell them. I'll deny it."

"What?" Galen eased me off his lap and got to his feet. "You'd lie for him?"

I hated the tone in his voice and what it implied. After the night we'd shared together, Galen had no reason to doubt my feelings for him.

But I was naked, and Maddox's scent was all over me. He was angry, protective and two of his senses were lying to him. Two senses we relied heavily upon as wolves. When they conflicted with what we knew as humans it messed with our heads.

I looked him straight in the eye. "No. But I would lie for *you*, Galen."

And more if it meant saving him from himself.

CHAPTER 14

GALEN

"Goddammit, Talia. I really can't leave you alone, can I?" I stormed into the bathroom, turned the faucet to hot and started the shower.

I came back out into the living area and closed the bathroom door behind me, letting the heat and steam build up in the small room, and proceeded to open every window in the cabin.

I was ready to explode, and Maddox's scent was fucking everywhere.

The cabin smelled like Maddox. Talia smelled like Maddox. His stench tainted everything and pushed my control right to the breaking point. I wanted to know what he'd done to her, but after I discovered the mark he'd made on her clavicle, rage overtook my mind.

Every rational thought I had was reduced to one simple fact. Maddox needed to be put down.

And it was my wolf that would do it.

Talia and Theo fought through my rage, hammering me with common sense until they were able to break through, past my wolf, and reach the man.

But I was hanging on by a thread and if I didn't clear Maddox's scent out of the cabin right now, I was going to lose my mind and do something stupid.

Like break the council's peace order and kill that privileged piece of shit.

Once Theo had scrubbed away the blood spatters on the floor, the air in the room cleared. Talia washed his scent from her body under the steaming hot shower, and finally my temper cooled a little to the point that I was able to think straight at last.

"Are you ready to listen now?" Talia stepped through the cloud of steam that followed her out of the bathroom.

Under different circumstances, a question like that might have plucked my nerves. But given the state I'd been in when I all but ordered her to take a shower, she had every right to ask if I was ready to hear what she had to say.

"Yeah. I am." I shook my head, distracted for an entirely different reason.

The thin silk robe clung to her damp skin and memories of the way she looked while we made love, her hair splayed around her like threads of spun gold, made it hard to concentrate on anything else.

"You sure?" She arched a quizzical brow; one corner of her mouth upturned in a knowing smile.

"Yeah, I'm good." I fisted my hand in front of my mouth, coughed and cleared my throat. "Listen, I'm sorr—"

"Don't." She cinched the rose-pink satin sash tight around her waist and padded across the room toward me. "You don't have anything to apologize for."

She sat beside me on the love seat while Theo took a seat opposite in the armchair.

"I know what happened is a trigger for you, Galen," Talia said. "Maddox must have figured it out too. Otherwise, he wouldn't have done it. Don't let him make this about Jessie because it isn't."

I winced at the mention of her name. Seeing Talia curled up and whimpering in front of the fire, blood spattered on the floor and Maddox's scent everywhere, had brought it all back. Every failure, my inability to protect both Jessie, and now Talia, had been shoved in my face.

"Galen, look at me." Talia's voice pulled me back from the darkest corners of my mind. "He's goading you and you can't let him. We need to forge alliances with the council and any pack willing to help us or we won't be able to stop the demons. That's what we came here to do, right?"

She reached for the cup of hot chocolate teaming with miniature marshmallows that Theo had made for her and popped one of the tiny pillowy confections into her mouth.

"Smart is a sexy look." I plucked the marshmallow she tossed at my head out of midair and dropped it in my own mug.

"Are you ready to hear what happened?"

At my nod, she settled more comfortably on the love seat. "After you and Theo left, I ran a hot bath and—"

"Maybe we should skip over any details involving you in a bubble bath," Theo interjected, looking vaguely uncomfortable.

"As much as it pains me to admit it, Theo has a point." I feigned a look of disappointment before shooting her a wink.

Talia was stronger than Maddox and the rest of the Northwood pack gave her credit for. Hell, she was stronger than me. After Jessie, I was a mess and hell bent on ruining my life for a long time. But not Talia. When life knocked her down, she just got right back up.

"As I was saying." She chuckled and shook her head. "Someone was jiggling the doorknob. I thought you had forgotten your key, so I went to check. It was Maddox."

I braced for the worst, secretly hoping that the truth would pale in comparison to what I imagined had happened to her.

"He started taunting me, using our history to bait me into an argument. When I informed him that he would never have the chance now to be my first…" She flicked her gaze at Theo; a slight blush reddened her cheeks. "He didn't like that at all and forced his way inside."

Talia had made a declaration about her feelings for me and our relationship. Granted it was to her ex, but she'd always held back when it came to taking the next step between her and me. The fact that she'd said it out loud to anyone—especially to Maddox—felt like a huge leap forward.

She recounted the rest of her ordeal, including the verbal exchange with Maddox, the physical altercation that led to him staking a claim on her as his property. That was a practice all but forbidden these days amongst the North American packs.

It shouldn't have come as a surprise that the Northwood pack was one that clung to old and barbaric practices that had no place in modern society.

Pride swelled in my chest when she described in vivid detail how she partially shifted her claws and slashed Maddox's face, after breaking his nose.

So, a lot of the blood spatter must have been his, not hers. No wonder the place had stunk of him.

"Son of a bitch didn't get half of what he deserved," Theo grumbled, mirroring my own thoughts. "But good for you. You spilled Maddox's blood, and the Northwood pack knows it."

"He'll try to claim what he thinks is owed to him." The ceramic mug cracked under my grip and hot chocolate seeped through the sides.

"Maybe not. He's only interested in hurting me to get to you." Talia set her mug on the coffee table and reached for mine, swapping out the cup for a napkin to dry my hands. "But I don't think he'll play that card until he absolutely has to."

I cringed inwardly over the irony of what she'd said. Talia had come into my life because I'd decided to kidnap her, to weaken Maddox, and use her as a bargaining chip.

It was a miracle that things had worked out the way they did. I couldn't imagine my life without Talia in it.

"So, what's our move?" Theo collected the blue and white speckled ceramic mugs and carried them to the kitchenette. "The summit is in full swing, and our dance card is full. Literally."

"Ugh, the ball is tonight, isn't it?" I groaned, rubbing my temples to stave off the headache forming behind my eyes.

"We could skip the extracurricular activities. Just focus on business." Theo returned with hot chocolate refills and the snack basket.

"No." Talia grabbed a chocolate-dipped peanut butter protein bar from the basket and peeled back the wrapper. "We need to act like nothing happened."

"Uh, I'm not sure if you two have met? Let me introduce you. Talia, this is Galen. He's an Alpha, protective by nature and occasionally hot headed." Theo jested, pointing his finger between me and Talia. "Acting like Maddox didn't just throw down the gauntlet of all gauntlets is going to be damn near impossible for him."

"Thank you for that overwhelming vote of confidence, Theo." I braced my elbows on my knees and rested my forehead against my fists. "You're both right."

Talia rubbed small, soothing circles across the middle of my back, and I leaned into her calming touch.

"I'm not saying that my temper won't get the best of me or that this won't end in disaster, but the lunar ball, the luncheons and cocktail hours, they're all part of the political chess game and we need to keep all our pieces on the board," I admitted.

Yet another reason why I hated politics.

My patience with the Northwood pack had worn thin a long

time ago. If it wasn't for the summit, my score with Maddox would be quickly settled. With his death.

But Maddox and his father weren't the only demons the Long Claw pack was up against.

The real deal legion from Hell had chosen our town as ground zero for their attack. It seemed Victor, the mysterious wolf from the north, had been right in his assumption that we were experiencing more demon activity than anywhere else in the country.

If my pack and the town we called home were going to survive, we needed as many packs on our side as we could.

The best way to do that wasn't attending the meetings. It was conversations over cocktails in a crowded ballroom and I dreaded every minute of it.

Theo felt the same way. After polishing off the last bag of beef jerky out of the snack basket, he headed up to the loft to shower and catch some sleep.

Talia and I had a few hours alone together before the ball and I knew exactly how I wanted to spend them.

But she'd just been assaulted by someone she used to love. Betrayed again by someone who was supposed to be her fated mate. The last thing she needed was a man coming on strong and taking control.

Whatever happened between us—if anything happened—I wanted Talia to initiate it. Our relationship needed to move at her pace, both emotionally and sexually.

It occurred to me at that moment how much I liked having her in control. Even if she never knew that she was.

I made decisions every day for the pack, about my father's medical care, for myself, and felt the weight of that power on my shoulders all the time. Still, it wasn't a burden. I loved my pack, and my father. I wanted to take care of them, but it felt good to have someone take care of me as well.

It felt even better not to be the one in charge, every once in a while.

I gave the authority in our relationship to Talia, confident that she wouldn't abuse the power I'd given her over me. She had stolen my heart. I handed her everything else.

"So." Talia tugged at the hem of the silk robe that clung to her curves.

"So," I repeated, draping my arm over the back of the loveseat in a silent invitation for her to move closer.

If she wanted to.

I wanted her to want to. But by not asking, I gave her the freedom to choose without any added pressure or fear of negative repercussions for the decision she made.

Talia held on to the bottom of her robe, scooched across the cushions and nestled against my side; her head resting on my chest. Her muscles relaxed and her breathing slowed as she slipped off to sleep.

I wrapped her in my arms, content just to hold her close, to feel her body next to mine. I would be content like this for the rest of my life. I wasn't the man I was when Talia and I first met; broken and barely holding the pieces of my shattered heart together.

She had healed me without even trying, and I wanted more than anything to do the same for her. With those thoughts in mind, I drifted off to sleep.

"Galen."

I opened my eyes, missing the warmth of Talia's body next to mine, as soon as I realized she wasn't curled up beside me.

"How long have I been asleep?" I twisted my head side to side, working out the kink in my neck from using the arm of the love seat as a pillow.

"A few hours." Talia came around the back of the couch, stood behind me and massaged my shoulders.

"Mmm." I moaned and tucked my chin against my chest, easing forward to give her better access to work her magic on my neck and shoulders.

"Better?" She leaned forward and planted a kiss on my temple.

"Like new." I took her right hand in mine, brought it to my lips and brushed a kiss against her palm. Then the scent hit me. "Is that coffee?"

I reached for the steaming mug resting on the coffee table in front of me.

"Coffee and a beautiful woman." I inhaled the rich, bitter-sweet notes of the freshly brewed cup and sighed. "The sun's barely up and my day is already off to an amazing start."

"Let's hope it stays that way." She ran her fingers through my hair, smoothing out my morning bedhead.

"We're at a demon summit. The odds of that happening aren't looking good." I leaned my head against the back of the couch, glanced up and gave a little wink. "But it's never really a bad day when I'm with you."

"You say that now, but the day's only just started. Talk to me the next time we're attacked by a demon or a ragey ex-boyfriend."

"How many ragey ex-boyfriends are we talking about?" I teased.

"From sweet to sass in six seconds flat." Talia's cerulean-violet eyes were as dazzling as her smile. "And to think, I plied you with coffee and worked out your kinks."

"There's an inappropriate joke there, but it's early and you did make coffee, so I'll give you a pass."

"Such a gentleman." Talia didn't skip a beat, teasing me right back.

We fell into an easy rhythm, enjoying each other's company and the start of what I hoped would be a peaceful day. After the night she'd had, she deserved it.

"What's on the agenda for today?" Talia dropped down beside me on the loveseat and draped her long, sculpted legs across my lap. "Are you meeting with the council again?"

"Nope. We don't have anything scheduled until the ball tonight. So, I'm all yours."

"Really?" She tapped her index finger against her lips. "However will we pass the time?"

"I'm sure you can think of something."

"There is one thing…" Talia moved her legs, crawled across the love seat to straddle my lap and draped her arms over my shoulders.

"You read my mind." I loosened the belt on her robe, opening the top and sliding it over her shoulders and down her arms to pool at her waist.

I skimmed my hands along her sides and around her hips to cup her ass, pressing her body against mine. She gasped and dropped her head back, exposing the length of her neck. I nuzzled behind her ear and kissed my way down her neck.

Her breath hitched and body went rigid when my lips found their way to her collar bone. And that notch.

"Galen, I—"

"Shit, Talia. I wasn't thinking." I sank back against the couch. "I'm sorry."

"Don't." Unshed tears glistened in her eyes. "Please don't say you're sorry."

She climbed off my lap, yanked her robe closed and collapsed on the cushion beside me.

"He's already taken so much from me. I can't let him steal this from me too."

I rested my hand on her collarbone, rubbing my thumb along the notch Maddox left when he marked her as his property.

"This doesn't mean anything," I said gently. "You're not his to claim." I took her hand and placed it over my heart. "You're mine. And I'm yours."

And I would do whatever it took to make sure she stayed that way.

CHAPTER 15

TALIA

Galen was everything I had ever wanted in a mate and more than I deserved. The closer we got, the harder it was to keep my secret from him. I needed to tell him the truth about my eyes, but it would have to wait until the summit ended.

When I was on familiar ground, safe behind the coven's wards on Long Claw pack land.

I didn't feel safe at the ranch. The sense of unease had started with the old woman at the reception dinner, and then our encounter with the Alaskan wolf Victor, and it had escalated after Maddox attacked me.

The only wolves I knew at the summit—other than Maddox and his father, of course—were Galen and Theo. If I told them the truth and they rejected me, there would be no one to help me.

I'd be completely alone.

At least I had one ally at home if things went south when Galen learned about my wolf's condition. Sarah would take me in until I was able to make arrangements with my aunt.

I hadn't thought about running since I found my way into the

Long Claw pack. Not after the demon branded my arm or the battle with my former Alpha and the Northwood Pack.

Not even after my red eyes appeared.

But Maddox changed everything when he carved a notch in my bone and staked his claim, not as my mate, but as my owner. Like I was a kept animal complete with collar and leash.

When I thought about it, it wasn't that much different when we were engaged. He made all the decisions. We did whatever made him happy. I was a kept woman even then. I just hadn't realized it at the time.

Galen showed me how different a relationship could be.

He listened to what I had to say, cared about the way I felt, and treated me like an equal. Not someone who was less than. I had a chance at happiness, a real future with a real partner, and that chance was slipping through my fingers like grains of sand.

Maddox would do anything to steal my happiness and he was succeeding. If he tried to claim me, there wasn't anyone who could stop him.

Except me—if I ran as far and as fast as I could.

The more I thought about what I needed to do, the better I felt. I had a plan. Or the workings of a plan.

Tell the truth. Await the fallout. Run if necessary.

I would lose my one chance at a happily ever after with Galen, but I would be alive on my own terms and not become Maddox's property.

It wasn't a perfect plan by any means, but it was the best one I had if things didn't turn out as I hoped once I'd shared my secret with Galen.

"Do you know how to tie one of these things?" Galen stood in the bathroom doorway, black bowtie in hand. He took one look at me and knew something was wrong. "Everything okay?"

He shoved the tie in his pants pocket, crossed the room and enveloped me in the warmth of his embrace. I molded my body to his, marveling at how perfectly we fit together, and wrapped my arms around his waist.

"It is now." I buried my face in his chest and held on for dear life.

He pulled back from our embrace and cupped my face in his hands, tracing the curve of my mouth with his thumb.

"Talia, there's something I need to say." His fingers trembled and his breathing quickened. "I wanted to tell you after we made love but was afraid you'd think that was the only reason I said it and then again last night but that didn't feel right either. But if I don't say it now, I'm afraid I won't have the courage to say it later. Talia, I—"

"Shush." I pressed my fingers against his lips, stopping the words from coming out of his mouth.

He couldn't say it yet. Not with the secret that lingered between us. When Galen spoke the words, when I heard him tell me he loved me for the first time, it had to be after I told him the truth and he knew everything about me.

Because, if he said it then, it would mean he truly loved me. The real me, warts and all. Right now, he didn't know everything about who and what I really was—I didn't even know that. So, I stopped him from saying it, even though my action hurt him and broke a little piece of my own heart.

I moved my hand from his mouth to his furrowed brow and smoothed the deepening crease between his eyebrows.

"Talia, what's wrong?" He took my hand in his, turning it to brush a kiss across my knuckles.

"Don't force it, Galen." I longed to hear the words he'd been so desperate to say, but I couldn't let him. Not yet. "You shouldn't have to muster up the courage to say it, and when the time is right, you won't have to."

"That's not what I meant when... Shit." The glimmer of hope in his eyes flickered and died. "I practiced this in my head a hundred times before I came out here and I still screwed it up."

"No, you didn't." I stood on tiptoe, pressed my lips to his and poured everything I felt for him into the kiss.

His hands roamed my back until he found the zipper pull on the back of my dress and eased it down.

"We'll be late," I warned, but my tone lacked conviction.

"It's called making an entrance." He bottomed out the zipper and slid his hands down the back of my dress to cup my bare ass.

"Theo could come barging in here any second."

That did the trick.

"I'm not going to lie; my pride is a little wounded." Galen rested his forehead against mine and kissed the tip of my nose.

"Anticipation, remember?" I slipped my hand in his pants pocket, brushing the length of his erection when I reached for his bowtie.

I took his tiny moan of pleasure as a promise of things to come.

THE BANQUET ROOM was filled to near capacity by the time we arrived. Servers navigated the room carrying champagne flutes on silver trays with the grace of ballroom dancers. A live band coaxed people out onto the parquet floor with covers of popular songs from the billboard charts.

Galen and Theo seemed content to stand on the sidelines and watch.

"I thought you said you needed to mingle." I clasped Galen's hand in mine and led him out onto the dance floor. "Come on."

"Mingling is not the same thing as dancing."

He looked toward Theo for help, but his Beta was in the process of being dragged onto the floor by a young woman from one of the Oregon packs.

The band slowed things down with a love song and the crowd thinned to couples only.

"See, this isn't so bad." I swayed my hips in time with the music and steered Galen around the floor, trying to make it look like he was steering me.

"I've never been much of a dancer." He stared at the floor, as if he was afraid he would crush my toes with one wrong step.

"Just follow my lead."

"I seem to be doing that a lot," he muttered, but when I looked up, he was grinning down at me with warmth in his eyes.

By the third song, Galen found his rhythm and relaxed enough to let the music move us around the floor.

"See, you're a natural." I rested my head on his shoulder and gave him the lead.

"I have a small confession to make." Galen grabbed my hand, spun me out, then snapped me in, tight against his body. His left hand splayed against the small of my back. "I'm not a bad dancer. Quite the opposite, in fact. It's just been a very long time since there was someone who made me want to dance."

He dipped me, low enough that my hair brushed the floor, and I questioned the ability of my dress's plunging neckline to hold everything in. With a firm tug, he pulled me back up, wrapped his arm around my waist and pulled me against him until our bodies molded together.

"Just follow my lead." With a quick kiss, and a smirk, he whisked me around the dance floor.

Other couples moved back, giving us the floor, and Galen used every inch of it. Several others who'd been seated at tables scattered around the room stepped forward to watch. A circle formed around the edge of the dance floor.

There were a few oohs and ahhs, and even a gasp, which truth be told, might have been from me, when Galen yanked me against him, grabbed my thigh and hitched my leg up on his hip.

The music ended and the lead singer of the band stepped up to the mic to announce they were taking a break. The musicians swapped places with a fresh-faced kid who looked to be in his late teens. He stepped behind a turntable, plugged in a beat maker and spun a track. The room erupted and a sea of bodies flooded the dance floor.

"I can't believe you know how to dance like that." I grabbed a champagne flute from a passing tray and gulped it down; the bubbles tickled my nose and throat. "You're like that guy in the movie from the eighties, you know the one, with the oldies music and the summer resort?"

"Where do you think I got my moves?" When I swapped out my empty glass for another full one, Galen grabbed the glass before I had a chance to take a sip. "Let's get you something hydrating first."

He grabbed a silver pitcher of ice water and two unused glasses from the nearest table and filled them to the brim.

"You're not serious about the movie? Are you?" I took a long sip of the ice water, studying his expression over the rim of the glass for any tells that he was lying. "Oh my God, you are serious."

"Of course, I'm serious." He finished the last sip of his water and poured himself another. "And to answer your question, yes. I can do the lift."

"I wasn't... I mean, that thought never crossed..." I stammered, fanning myself as I thought about the scene in the movie and the way the actor held his partner in his arms, and the way her body slid against his as he lowered her slowly back to the floor.

Galen set his empty glass on a nearby table and cocked his head to one side as he eyed the aisle between tables.

"We've got room. Want to try it?" A slight dimple formed on his cheek.

"In these heels?" I laughed. "I'll break my ankle before I run three steps in your direction."

"Want to get some air?" He paused, as if he'd reconsidered his suggestion. "Actually, it's freezing outside. How about we grab a table for two in a dark corner."

"We could go back to the cabin." I trailed my hands down the buttons of his dress shirt, stopping short when I reached the waistband of his pants.

"We could." Galen leaned in and kissed me until my knees buckled and I was out of breath. "Let me find Theo and let him know we're skipping out early."

He scanned the room in search of his Beta, laughing when he finally found him in the crowd of people swaying on the dance floor.

"I think he's going to be just fine on his own." Galen pointed toward Theo who was surrounded by a small harem of women, all vying for his attention.

Theo had the superhero looks, a sense of humor and status in a pack that women went crazy for. Any one of the women hanging on his every word would have been lucky to have him. He was a genuinely nice guy. The total package.

But I had a thing for Alphas. One in particular.

Galen took my hand in his, weaving us through the crowded room, toward the exit.

"Oh, excuse me." A silver-haired man apologized for bumping Galen with the crook of his cane as he shuffled his way through the crowd. "I didn't mean to... You're Max's boy, aren't you?"

"I am."

Galen beamed at the mention of his father. He was proud to be Max's son. He'd been a good Alpha and an even better dad, and I envied their relationship.

"I'm sorry; have we met?" Galen studied the man's face. "If we have, it's my turn to apologize, because I don't remember."

"I'd be surprised if you did. You were just a pup the last time I saw you." The old man extended his hand.

His fingers were knobby and crooked from arthritis, one of the few mundane ailments that affected shifters as well, on account of the number of times our bones dislocated or having been broken too many times. Considering his likely age, and the number of challenges he must have survived, my money was on the latter.

"My name is Eli Whitaker." The old man scanned the room. 'Where is the old man? I haven't seen Max in ages."

"He wasn't able to attend the summit and sent me in his place."

"Nothing serious, I hope." Eli studied Galen's reaction and let out a sigh when he'd made his deduction. "I see. Walk me to my table, son. You don't mind if I steal him away from you, for a moment?"

Reality crept back into our night, siphoning the magic we'd made on the dance floor. For a moment the troubles at home had seemed a lifetime away.

Eli hadn't meant to dampen our spirits or darken our evening. There was no way he could have known about Max's condition. Galen forbade anyone in the Long Claw pack to speak of it outside of the pack.

"Not at all." I pointed to an empty table halfway between the dance floor and the door. "I'll just wait over there."

Galen shook his head and pointed to another table with a clear line of sight from Eli's table. He wanted to keep an eye on me. Had I not been marked by a demon and a shifter, I might not have found his overprotectiveness quite so endearing.

Of course, with my knack for getting in trouble, his concern wasn't unwarranted.

"May I have this dance?" The familiar cadence of the gravelly male voice behind me turned my stomach and sent shivers down my spine.

"No." I refused to formally acknowledge Maddox's father's presence or even so much as glance in his direction.

"No? You think playing pretend with the Alpha from the Long Claw pack gives you authority to refuse me?"

He leaned in close, his breath hot against the back of my neck.

"The mark you bear from my son is bone deep and says otherwise. You're the property of the Northwood pack and mine to do with as I see fit. So, how about you not make a scene for once and do as you're fucking told?"

He gripped my arm, in almost the same spot his son had, and clamped down, pressing his fingertips into my bicep. I felt the slight prick of a claw through the fabric of my dress and knew if I tried to fight, he'd shred my arm to pieces.

"Move your ass." He shoved me toward the dance floor but kept hold of my arm.

The heel of my stiletto snagged on the carpet, causing me to trip and jar my ankle. I wobbled and almost went down to my knees, but my old Alpha yanked me up and forced me to walk, putting weight on my injured foot.

"You know, your mom had a mark gouged out of her bone just like that." He nodded toward my collar bone, and seized my hand in his vice-like grip, crushing my knuckles together.

"Never understood why your father went dumpster diving for that one. Told him to take out the trash before he got himself in too deep, but he never listened. Might still be alive today if he had."

"He'd still be alive if you weren't a cold-blooded murder."

He dug his fingers into my side like he was performing arthroscopic surgery and in search of my appendix.

"You really ought to be nicer to me and the heir to my throne. I could snap your neck right here, drop your dead body in the middle of this dance floor and nobody would lift a finger to stop me."

"The council would. You can't break the summit peace order."

"See," he sucked the word and a mouthful of air through his teeth. "This is why we don't let women get involved in politics.

The peace order is between packs. I can do whatever I want, when I want, wherever I want, with my own property. And that includes at this summit.

"Good thing you're pretty, 'cause you're not very smart. That's why we're keeping you for breeding. Well, not for actual breeding. More for practice, if you catch my meaning. I can't have your genes tainting the future of my pack, can I?"

"There's nothing wrong with my genes. My parents were Northwood, no different from you." I feigned confidence that I didn't feel and spat the words in his face.

The truth hurt and his words hit close to home. There was something wrong with me. But it had nothing to do with my genes or who my parents were.

Unless he knew something I didn't.

Which was entirely possible. I was young when we lost my mother and my father preferred to bury his pain and her memories at the bottom of a bottle of booze. We never talked about her.

What if I was like her? The people of Northwood sure seemed to think so. And if I was, what did that actually mean?

CHAPTER 16

GALEN

"Mind if I cut in?" I managed to control my seething temper long enough to poke the Northwood asshole senior in the shoulder. "I think you've had her quite long enough."

I knew he wouldn't refuse me. He couldn't. There were too many witnesses. Too many people who'd not only seen Talia and me in an intimate dance routine together, but knew she was a registered guest at the summit under the Long Claw pack.

His son may have notched her bone, leaving his mark, but he'd failed to announce the claim to the council or anyone else, if the glares and accusatory looks were any indication.

I didn't need to lay claim to her bones, because I'd staked my claim on her heart. Publicly.

And unlike Junior, sulking in the corner, I had Talia's permission.

He pivoted on his heel, turning them on the dance floor, and sneered over Talia's shoulder when he came to face me.

"You're pretty smug for an old man who got his ass handed to him the last time he crossed paths with her." I dipped my head in a gesture toward Talia. "Something tells me you're lucky the council instituted a peace order over the summit, or she'd kick your ass again."

"Please, you honestly think she could take me in a fight?" The Alpha scoffed. "I let her win. Every move I make is a calculated one. It led me here, with her under my thumb, a nice little bargaining chip, wouldn't you say?"

Damn. How many times would that come back to haunt me? Once was too many. I wasn't proud of what I'd done, snatching Talia the way I had for my pack's gain. I'd apologized. She'd accepted.

I still planned to spend the rest of my life making it up to her.

"If you or your son think of laying a hand on her again, I will end you both. We won't have to negotiate her release, because the only thing we'll be negotiating are the terms for a challenge."

"I welcome it." He gripped Talia by the shoulders, shoved her backward and stalked off the parquet floor.

I braced for impact, caught Talia in my arms and swept her off the floor toward the door.

"Did you just challenge the Northwood Alpha?" Talia gaped at me as I pulled out the valet ticket and handed it over to the young woman working the kiosk. "How are you so calm right now?"

"He's grasping at straws. He didn't plan any of this." I rested my hand at the small of her back and guided her toward the UTV when it pulled up to the curb.

The driver hopped out from behind the wheel, rushing off to help the next guest, but I managed to slip her a twenty before she disappeared.

"The summit provided an opportunity to get close to you, but he didn't know for certain you'd be here," I added.

"That still sounds like he kind of planned it. The attack at the cabin, at least." Talia reached around the back of her seat and grabbed the fleece blanket folded on the small rear passenger seat.

"No, Maddox screwed up and his dad is trying to make the best of it."

I pressed the gas pedal and veered onto the path that led us back to Harrier House.

"Maddox came to the cabin to mess with you and bait me into a fight. No question about it. You were right about that. But he didn't count on you getting the better of him and goading him into attacking you."

"I didn't do it on purpose."

"I know, sweetheart." I gripped the steering wheel with my left hand and reached over with my right to pull the blanket up over her shoulders. "I'm sorry. I didn't mean to insinuate that you did."

She grabbed my hand before I could move it away and held on, lacing her fingers through mine.

"What I meant was, neither of them accounted for you sticking up for yourself. That pissed Maddox off and he forced entry into our cabin and attacked you."

I slowed the UTV and eased it onto the small concrete pad on the side of the cabin.

"All of that happened before he went archaic and notched your bone. And they are underestimating you again. They think you'll be so humiliated that your fated mate rejected you and then reclaimed you, not as his bride but as his property, that you'll keep your mouth shut."

I winced when I said the last part out loud. It sounded harsh even to me and I hadn't meant it to be. It was the truth, but I should have found a way to soften the delivery.

To Talia's credit, she took it in stride.

"You want me to say something to the council." Talia tightened her grip on my hand and shook her head. "Not if you're going to use that as an opportunity to challenge him."

"Maddox screwed up, big time. I'm not going to waste this kind of leverage on a challenge. I can do that any time I want."

Talia cocked her head to one side and narrowed her eyes, a confused look on her face.

"Northwood had officially broken ties with you, and you were already Long Claw when he attacked you. Maddox broke the peace order. They're using the bone mark as a cover. But any one of the council members will be able to date the notch."

"In other words, they're screwed."

"Yes, well and truly." Her smile was infectious. I couldn't help but match hers with one of my own, and she hadn't even heard the best part. "But wait, there's more. We can play this out two ways. Go to the council, tell them what Maddox did and leave his fate up to them, or we blackmail Northwood to remove the claim on you."

"Why can't we tell the council and force him to remove the mark?"

I didn't expect her to know all the rules and regulations. Unlike the women in the Long Claw pack, Talia and the others in her old pack had been excluded from policy and politics. They were in the dark and had no say in the laws that governed them.

"As barbaric as it is, the claim is binding. The council will have to recognize it. So, it won't matter when the mark happened. Just that it happened. Northwood could still claim you for his pack regardless of what punishment the council doled out on Maddox."

"Blackmail it is." Her smile faltered as she glanced out the thick plastic window. "It's crazy how much my life has changed in just a few weeks."

"Any regrets?" I asked, unsure if I wanted to hear her answer.

What if she regretted staying with me and my pack instead of splitting town to live with her aunt like she'd planned?

"You mean besides these stilettos? Just how much of my life I wasted being a sheep, instead of a wolf?" Talia shifted in the passenger seat and turned to face me. "I don't ever want to be kept in the dark again."

"You won't be. I promise." I killed the engine and pulled the key from the ignition. "Come on, there's a fire and a soaker tub inside with our names on them."

Talia was out of the UTV and in the cabin before I unbuckled my seat belt.

A trail of clothes and shoes led from the door to the soaker tub. She stripped out of her dress, kicked off her shoes and removed all of her jewelry except the bracelet Sarah gave her before we left for the summit.

"Bubbles or no bubbles?" Talia sat on the edge of the tub in a sheer lace demi bra and thong that left nothing to the imagination.

I let out a low whistle.

"Forget the bath." I undid my bowtie and tossed it, along with my tuxedo jacket, on the couch.

Talia swiveled on the tub's edge, turning toward me, and uncrossed her legs. She left the most sensitive and sacred part of her body exposed just long enough to tease.

"Fuck me." I muttered almost under my breath, unbuttoning my shirt as fast as I could.

"Oh, I intend to." Talia pushed off the edge of the tub and stalked across the room.

She removed my diamond cufflinks, slipped them in my pants pocket and yanked off the dress shirt. Her hands replaced mine at my waistband. She unfastened my pants, undid the zipper and let them fall down around my ankles.

She ran her hand along the length of my shaft, stroking, teasing, pushing me toward climax. I knew I would last long if she kept that up.

"Talia, you're driving me crazy."

She started to kneel, but I grabbed her by her elbows, eased her back to her feet, gripped her waist and hoisted her up. She wrapped her legs around my hips and locked them together at the ankles behind my back.

Pants still wrapped around my ankles, I duck-walked toward the bed, where I intended to throw her on the mattress and ravish her for hours.

But we didn't quite make it that far.

At a particularly loud moan from her I hitched her up on my hips, pressed her back against the wall and slid her lace panties out of the way. She was so tight. I eased inside. I could have come right then, but I took it slow. I buried myself inside her, ground my hips against hers and let the pressure build for both of us.

Talia dug her nails in my back and bit down on my shoulder, stifling her moans of pleasure as I took her right there in the living room.

We finally made it to the bed, collapsing beside each other on the mattress. Talia inched her way over to my side, nestled into a spooning position and pulled the covers up and over both of us.

"Why didn't you say something about getting Maddox to revoke his claim earlier?" Talia stifled a yawn and tugged my arm over her waist.

"Honestly, it didn't even occur to me until tonight. My temper has been at a simmer since last night and I haven't been thinking as clearly as I should."

I tucked an errant strand of her golden-red locks behind her ear and ran my fingers down the length, twirling the end around my finger.

"When I saw Northwood roughing you up on the dance floor, I had every intention of kicking his ass in front of everyone—including the council—and it just sort of hit me."

"You're always looking out for me, protecting me. I've never really had that before. Not with Maddox, not even with my father. The pack always came first." She covered her mouth with the back of her hand and gave in to the yawn she'd been fighting back. "Galen?"

"Yes, Talia?"

"I think I'm in love with you."

"I know I'm in love with you." My response fell from my lips without hesitation.

Only to be met with soft snores from the woman who would be my future mate.

Talia wasn't awake to hear me tell her I loved her, but she knew. I'd tried to tell her earlier and she stopped me. She didn't want me to feel pressured or obligated into saying it. I tried to reassure her that it wasn't either of those things.

Talia seemed to still have reservations. I think I'm in love with you wasn't quite the same as I am in love with you. It wasn't an outright declaration of her love for me, but she came close.

And that was good enough for me. For now.

I knew she would say the words in her own time, when she was ready, and I was more than willing to wait.

Because I was and always would be in love with Talia Linetti.

CHAPTER 17

TALIA

Galen left shortly after sunrise for an ungodly early morning meeting. How anyone could navigate putting on clothes and brushing their teeth at that hour, never mind the intricate details of pack politics, was beyond me.

He didn't want to wake me, opting for a bedside note to let me know when he'd return and that there was a fresh pot of coffee waiting for me in the kitchenette.

I was grateful he'd chosen to let me sleep in. After the highs and lows of the previous night, my body needed as many additional hours of REM as it could get.

Muscles I hadn't known existed ached from a night of dancing and romancing. But it wasn't the physical exertion on the dance floor and in the bedroom that left me exhausted, it was the emotional warfare Maddox and his father used against me.

Still, Galen had given me one of the most amazing nights of my life and I'd ended it by saying I thought I loved him.

I came as close as I could to admitting my true feelings for him without actually saying the words, I love you. It felt wrong saying them without having shared all of my secrets with him.

You don't lie to people you love. Because if they really love you back, they have accepted you at your best and your worst.

That was how I knew Maddox had never truly loved me.

And why I was so afraid to tell Galen about my red wolf eyes. I knew that I couldn't handle that sort of rejection again.

So, I closed my eyes and pretended to be asleep when he declared his love for me. Hearing him say it out loud meant the world to me. It took everything I had not to wrap my arms around him and profess my love, but doing so would have opened the door to a conversation I wasn't ready to have.

Especially while I still bore Maddox's mark.

The thought of being their property, used and abused by the Northwood pack, terrified me more than I cared to admit.

Galen came up with a brilliant plan to force Maddox to revoke his claim on me. And as manipulative as it sounded, that was one more reason I needed to wait to tell Galen about my eyes.

I pushed away the negative thoughts and crippling doubts that crept into my mind and forced myself to get out of bed. It looked like another beautiful day on the ranch, and I wanted to spend some of it outside.

I'd skipped every run for obvious reasons and had spent too much time indoors.

After a quick pit stop in the bathroom, I poured myself a cup of coffee and planned out my day. The first order of business was a long hot shower to loosen my cramped muscles. Second, was a nature hike. I saw walking trails, varying in difficulty, in the ranch's brochure and couldn't wait to get out there and do a little exploring.

I sent Galen a brief text to share my plans for the day, along with which hiking trails I wanted to check out, and waited for his reply before I jumped in the shower.

Have fun. Be safe. Love you. Galen was still in his meeting and kept his text short and sweet.

My day had been greenlit. I hurried into the shower before he changed his mind and deemed walking alone an unsafe activity.

In his defense, it probably was.

I'd considered asking Theo to join me, knowing full well he was still up in the loft sleeping, but decided against it. The paths I'd chosen to explore weren't far from the cabin and the two largest threats to my existence would be at the same meeting as Galen.

A hot shower was just what I needed. I stayed beneath the rainfall showerhead until the water ran cold and dressed in a pair of fleece-lined leggings, a thick, oversized sweatshirt on top of a long-sleeved tee shirt and hiking boots.

I packed a water bottle and a couple of protein bars then headed out for the Catamount trail with the hopes that I didn't run into its namesake.

The trail ran through the eastern valley, cut through a pine forest and looped back around through a wildflower meadow on the western side of the ranch. Round trip, I planned to be gone for a few hours.

That was before I crossed paths with the old woman from the welcome dinner two nights before.

It seemed an odd coincidence—assuming I believed in coincidence, which I didn't—that we would run into each other out in the middle of nowhere.

She wasn't an Alpha, or she would have been at the meeting with Galen, but that didn't mean she wasn't strong or high ranking within her own pack.

A wolf didn't live to her age by being weak.

She was headed straight for me, so I stepped off the trail into ankle high scrub brush and yielded the path, giving her plenty of room to navigate the incline with her walking stick.

Her silver hair was pulled back in a fishtail braid that cascaded down her back, with long wisps of hair around her face and crown escaping the braid.

She was dressed in comfortable clothes, a navy-blue long sleeve thermal, loose khaki colored cargo pants and a puffy burgundy vest zipped over the top.

"You're with the Long Claw pack, aren't you?" She stopped across from me and leaned on a locust wood walking stick that was twice as long as she was tall.

"Yes, ma'am. I sure am." I walked alongside through the brush and hopped back on the worn trail only once I'd passed her.

"Then why are the Northwoods so interested in you?" She tilted her head to the side, brows arched as she awaited my answer.

"I'm sorry? Have we met? Maybe you know someone from my family? I'm a Linetti."

"Linetti. Lin-net-ti." She rolled my last name around in her mouth like a sommelier sampling a fine wine. "Nope. The name doesn't ring any bells."

"Well, I'm afraid you have me at a bit of a disadvantage. You already know a few things about me, and I don't know anything about you. Which pack are you attending the summit with?"

"Mount Bona."

I knew it wasn't a coincidence. "Really?" I asked, feigning surprise. "I met a packmate of yours, Victor..." I snapped my fingers. "Victor something...What was his last name?

"Curry. Victor Curry." She knew who he was.

Just as I suspected.

Victor's run in with Galen and I hadn't been a coincidence either. Theo hadn't been able to find any information on the two of them. There was nothing in the ranch's guest registration. Victor was a no show at the poker game, and the old woman had given him the slip when he tailed her.

If we hadn't seen them with our own eyes, we never would have known they existed, never mind attended the council summit. They stayed off everyone's radar and didn't draw attention to themselves unless there was something they wanted you to see.

What was it that Victor and the old woman wanted us to know? I had no idea, but neither of us were leaving the forest until I found out what it was.

"Yes, that's him. He seems like a nice guy." I rested my hands on my hips and cocked my head to one side. "And you are?"

"Valerie Whitlock." She extended her hand in an official greeting.

"Nice to meet you, Valerie." I stepped forward and shook her hand, unsure if what I'd said was true.

The jury was still out. I was zero-for-three when it came to interactions with summit guests outside Galen and Theo. Still, if she didn't threaten, attack, or mark me, I would consider it a win.

"You never answered my question." Valerie had a firm grip and held our handshake longer than necessary. She released me when she caught me staring at our clasped hands. "Why are the Northwoods so interested in you?"

"I could ask the same of you and Victor. You were staring at me all through the dinner the other night. Don't bother denying it now, because you certainly weren't being discreet about it during dessert. And then we just happened to bump into a pack mate of yours on our way out of the banquet hall."

Valerie smiled as if she were pleased that I had put two and two together.

"So, quid pro quo, Valerie. I will tell you about the Northwood pack and you tell me what you and Victor want with me. This way I can get a handle on my friends and foes and prioritize the trouble headed my way."

"You don't have anything to fear from me or Victor. It costs me nothing to agree to those terms."

"Fine." I crossed my arms over my chest and shifted my weight to my other leg. "I used to be part of the Northwood pack."

"Used to be. It's unusual for a woman with your physical attributes and of breeding age to leave her pack. This wasn't by your choice?" Valerie agreed to the terms I'd set for our conversation, but I wasn't sure she understood them.

"Nope, it's my turn, Valerie. Why are you and Victor so interested in me?"

"You remind us of a wolf we lost a long time ago. Victor pointed you out during dinner and I have to admit, the resemblance is uncanny. But it was clear you weren't her. It was rude of me to stare."

Valerie reached for something on her hip. I couldn't see whether it was a weapon or not, but I wasn't taking any chances. I tucked my elbows in, shifted my weight to my right foot and got ready to make a run for it.

"Relax, Talia." She held up a clear refillable water bottle. "You've got some trust issues. Whatever caused the split with you and Northwood isn't water under the bridge, is it?"

"Let's just say there's a lot of blood in that water."

"Interesting." She narrowed her gaze and sized me up. "They disowned you, didn't they?"

I'd already lost track of where we were in the give and take. Valerie was better at quid pro quo than I was. It was pretty obvious she'd played before.

"My mother was from a pack up north. Was she the woman you lost? Is she who I remind you of?"

"I already told you, Linetti doesn't ring any bells. It was a case of mistaken identity. Nothing more."

"I'm not buying it." I leaned against the trunk of a pine tree, unhooked my water from my belt loop and took a long sip. "You and I wouldn't have run into each other today if it was just a case of mistaken identity. You've been keeping tabs on me, waiting until another opportunity presented itself to catch me alone."

"I can see why you have trust issues, after being raised in the

Northwood pack, but I assure you, Victor and I have no interest in causing you trouble or harm."

"If that's true, it would sure be a nice change of pace."

I couldn't explain why, because there was no rational explanation for it beyond a gut feeling, but I wanted to believe her. I wanted to trust her.

"The Northwood boy, he claimed you?" Her gaze dropped to the collar of my hoodie. "His father casts you out and then he finds a way to reel you back in."

My gasp confirmed her theory.

"How did you know that? Were you watching when he attacked me?" My temper flared. Had she seen the whole thing and done nothing to intervene?

"When you're as old as I am, Talia, you learn to sense these things. A bone claim is an old tradition. It's not practiced any more, but when I was a little girl, it was a vital part of pack law. A way to keep unmated women in the pack. You learn to recognize the magic in the bond. To be honest, I'm surprised the Northwood boy knew about it."

"Me too, though I suppose I shouldn't be."

"Now that we're acquainted, perhaps we could walk together? These old bones lock up if I stand in one place too long." She motioned down the path in the direction I'd been headed. "You said your mother was from a northern pack. I take it Linetti wasn't her given name?"

"No, she met my father and joined the Northwood pack after they were married." I fell into step beside her on the path.

"What's her maiden name? The northern packs, like Mount Bona, tend to be smaller. The terrain isn't as forgiving, and limited resources means smaller numbers. Plus, people seem to hate cold weather." She hooked her water bottle back on her belt.

"I don't know."

"What about her pack name, do you know that?" Valerie

pressed me for information that would help her figure out if she knew my mother, but it was pointless.

It's hard to give someone information that you never had to begin with.

"She died when I was young. I barely remember what she looked like, and my father never talked about her. It was too painful for him."

"Well, maybe you could give him a call. See if he'll talk about her this once." Valerie switched her walking stick to her left hand. "It's worth a shot. I mean, what are the odds we'll ever see each other outside of the summit?"

I had a sneaking suspicion the odds were pretty good. Valerie was as interested in learning more about my mother as I was.

"I would, but he's dead."

"Oh, my condolences dear." Valerie rested her hand on my shoulder and gave it a comforting squeeze. "You have no family to speak of?"

"I have Galen and the Long Claw pack. They're my family now."

"Good, it's important for a girl to have roots." Valerie glanced up at the sun. "I'd say it's time for you to be getting back to that beau of yours."

"We're meeting for lunch. It's early yet. I have plenty of time before I need to..." I pulled my phone out of my pocket and checked the time. "You're right, I need to get back. How is that even possible?"

"Time flies when you're with good company. I'll talk with Victor. Maybe he will recognize your father's name and can trace it back to your mother."

Valerie balanced her walking stick against her shoulder and clasped my hand between hers.

"I enjoyed talking with you today, Talia."

She released my hand, stepped off the path and disappeared into the woods.

How the hell did she do that? It looked like I was going to have to stop teasing Theo about an old woman giving him the slip.

I double-timed it back to the cabin before Galen could assume the worst and send out a search party.

I couldn't wait to share what I'd learned—or not learned. The lack of information I'd acquired seemed as important as the information I did get.

Which, admittedly, wasn't much.

Still, we knew who she was and what pack she belonged to. We also knew she wasn't an enemy.

Which meant she could potentially be an ally. Something of which we were in short supply. We couldn't defeat the demons on our own. We needed all the allies we could get.

We needed a wolf like Valerie.

CHAPTER 18

GALEN

Talia still hadn't returned from her hike when I got back to the cabin to pick her up for lunch and the closing ceremonies. I glanced at my watch and talked myself, and my wolf, off a ledge.

She was five minutes late.

That was nothing, hardly enough time to send me into a panic and organize a search and rescue mission.

Still, this was Talia and, as proven on multiple occasions, trouble followed her everywhere.

She could defend herself. I'd seen her fight, but the peace order put all of us in a precarious situation. You had to calculate whether the argument was worth coming to blows over, and in a fight, those calculations cost precious seconds.

I decided to give her a few more minutes and used the quiet time to call home and check in on my dad.

David answered. My father was sleeping. I didn't want to wake him and used the time to bring my Beta up to speed on the summit, where we stood with the demons, and the few allies I had managed to convince to help us.

Talia emerged from the pines and crested the hill just as I was filling David in on the other events at the summit—namely the ones involving the Northwood pack.

Things had escalated.

I'd hoped to return home with at least one problem resolved. But even with the council orchestrating a unification the likes of which I've never seen before, the fight was still at a local level and there weren't enough wolves to go around.

All of the packs were stretched thin.

"Hey, handsome." Talia smiled and waved as she abandoned the path and cut across the grass. Sorry I'm late. I didn't mean to worry you."

"I wasn't worried." I tried to play it cool, but she saw right through me.

"Good, because we have a lot to catch up on over lunch and I need you level-headed. I'm just going to use the bathroom and then we can head out." Talia grabbed the key to unlock the cabin out of my hand.

"Something happened." I closed my eyes and shook my head. Anger and frustration twisted my expression and curled my hands into fists at my side. "I knew it."

"Nothing bad happened. It's just information I need to share with you, but I really have to pee first."

Patience wasn't exactly my strong suit. I followed her into the cabin and questioned her from my side of the bathroom door.

Her answer about meeting Valerie was the last thing I expected.

"You mean, it had nothing to do with the Northwood pack?"

I found it hard to believe Maddox hadn't used the Alpha only morning meeting to his advantage and harassed Talia once more before the summit wound down.

"Not really. At least not in the way that you mean." Talia shrugged. "Valerie asked about the Northwood pack. She seemed interested in why I wasn't a member anymore, but other than that, no. No sign of Maddox or their third."

"It's a bit strange, her watching you the way she has been, but if she wanted to hurt you, I believe she would have done it by now. It's not like she hasn't had the opportunity."

Talia and I locked up the cabin and waited for Theo outside.

"Who's hurting who, now?" He skipped the last few steps, vaulted himself over the railing and stuck the landing in the grassy side yard.

"Talia found your mark. Had a nice little chat with her, too." I unzipped the plastic door and helped Talia inside the UTV.

"What? No, she didn't. There's no way." Theo continued to grumble his disbelief as he climbed into the back seat.

Talia filled him in on what had happened during her hike while I split my focus from driving to the luncheon, to listening to her retell her encounter with the old woman for any details I might have missed the first time I heard it.

"Mount Bona, huh? That pack is pretty far north." Theo rested his forearms against the backs of our seats and leaned in until his upper body occupied what little space there was between the two front seats. "And that Victor guy is a member of her pack too? We called that one."

"I think we can convince them to help us. The demons haven't moved that far north. She said the packs there are small, but I'm sure they have some wolves who would be willing to help us," Talia said.

Talia was an optimist. I envied her ability to see the bright side or at least find the silver lining. I hoped she was right about Valerie and Victor.

We needed all the help we could get.

We arrived at the banquet hall to find a memo taped to the front door. The luncheon had been canceled and the closing ceremony moved up.

A legion of demons had attacked a neighboring town. The Alphas who lived in the region had asked the council for help and in an unprecedented show of good faith they agreed.

Lead by example. It was something my father taught me before I could hunt on my own and had long been in practice in our pack.

But it was a first for the council. Their leadership style had always been more of a 'do as I say, not as I do' approach.

Still, the council stepping off their dais to help another packed boded well for the rest of us.

We hopped back into the UTV and headed over to the ceremonial grounds where the rest of the attendees had already gathered.

"Ladies and gentlemen," Jarica said. "We called this summit to create a safe place for the North American packs to come together and form the necessary alliances to defeat the greatest enemy we have ever faced and now the devil is at our doorstep."

Jarica stood beneath two massive pine trees, whose branches meshed together to create an emerald-green canopy above her head.

Hushed voices intensified, and the crowd grew restless with the news that demons were closing in on the council as well.

"Who will help us? Who will stand with their brothers and sisters to fight the demons and strike a blow to our enemy?"

The crowd erupted. Hands shot up, and men and women could be heard shouting their commitment to the local packs.

I never would have believed it if I hadn't witnessed it for myself.

"In light of events happening in two nearby towns, we gathered you here for the closing ceremonies and unification run. We are asking you to take an oath, to your pack, to your neighbors' pack, and to the council."

She pointed to a fellow councilman who also served as shaman and spiritual advisor to the alliance and its pack members.

He nodded and stepped forward. "It is time for the oath." The shaman raised his arms above his head. "Brothers and sisters, call forth your wolf. Let us seal this union in our truest forms. One pack, one wolf."

"One pack, one wolf." The crowd repeated the shaman's words.

"One pack, one wolf." He said them again, and again.

And again, the men and women gathered among the pines raised their voices and repeated his words.

Alphas and their pack representatives all around us shifted to their wolf form. It was the largest pack of wolves I'd ever seen in one place. It took my breath away and gave me hope for the future.

I hated politics, but this? Wolf helping wolf, that was something I could get behind.

I tapped the pack bond and nudged an added boost of power to Talia and Theo to accelerate the shift without the painful physical side effects.

Theo dropped to all fours and howled with the other wolves who had completed their shift.

"I don't want to." Talia backed away from the ceremony. "I don't want to do this. Don't make me do this, Galen." Her voice was panicked.

"What? What are you talking about? You don't want to do this?" I grabbed her shoulders and held her in place. "You have to do this, Talia. It's not an option. We have to shift to show our unity to the council and our allies. We need our allies, Talia. Please."

"Galen, I can't. You don't understand."

Theo whimpered, sat on his haunches and watched our argument unfold.

"Then help me understand, Talia. You haven't shifted with

a pack in days. Not just here, but at home. With your family. Tell me what's wrong."

I was finally going to have an answer for what had been bothering her. Something other than she wasn't feeling well or had another migraine coming on.

And then Northwood spoke up and drew the council's attention to Talia.

"She refuses to shift?" His booming voice carried over the crowd, silencing the others in attendance. "She rejects the alliance and her pack."

"No, that's not true. I... It's just..." Talia stammered, unable to string a coherent defense together for herself.

Valerie and Victor stood on the edge of the crowd which had morphed into an angry mob of wolves and men. They seemed to be waiting for something. What it was, I had no clue.

Talia needed their help.

She'd hoped they would be our allies, but if they wouldn't step forward and help her defend herself from a pack of angry wolves, it didn't bode well for their help defending the Long Claw pack from demons.

"Galen, please." Her gaze pleaded with me to do something, anything, to help her.

The fear in her eyes was more than my wolf and I could bear. He scratched and clawed his way to the surface, ready to rip himself free of my body to defend his mate.

My wolf was strong. One on one, there weren't many wolves at the summit I would hesitate to challenge.

But we couldn't take them all at once.

"Enough." Jarica growled into her bullhorn and brought the mob to heel. "Galen, from the Long Claw pack, step forward."

The crowd parted, forming a narrow aisle for me to walk.

"Councilwoman." I steeled my nerves and my spine and stood at my full height before her.

"I don't know what is going on with your packmate, but I have other, more important news to share with you."

"What could be more important than this?" I hadn't meant to say it out loud. That last thing I wanted to do was try her patience and press my luck.

"Your father passed away a few minutes ago."

I jerked at her announcement.

She rested her hand on my shoulder and squeezed. "I am so sorry. Brothers and sisters." Jarica called the attention of the crowd away from Talia to me. "Max Long Claw has died. He served this council well for many years and was a friend and ally to many of you here today. Bow your heads for a moment of silence."

The crowd obeyed her command. People in their human forms clasped their hands together in front of them and dipped their heads. Wolves lay on the ground and covered their muzzle with their front paws.

I'd just called David to check in on my father.

He hadn't gotten any better, but he hadn't gotten any worse. He was as fine as he could be and was taking a nap. Wasn't he?

It wasn't possible. There had to be a mistake. My father couldn't be dead. I would know it. I would feel it.

A son would know something like that, and I felt nothing. So, he had to still be alive.

Talia pushed her way through the crowd and took me in her arms. Her violent sobs shook my body and tears soaked through my shirt.

"Galen Long Claw ascends the throne." Jarica spoke to the crowd and then directed her next statement to me. "Go home, make arrangements and unify your people. I will be in touch."

Theo padded up alongside me, nudging my leg with his nose and whining. I couldn't think, couldn't move. My brain switched over to autopilot.

Talia led me back to the UTV and drove us to the cabin. She

packed everything and made all the arrangements for our return trip.

Important details that I cared nothing about.

My father was dead.

It was time for me to stop playing pretend and be the man, the Alpha, my father had raised me to be.

But the honest truth was, I didn't want the job or the responsibilities he left me.

I just wanted my father back.

CHAPTER 19

TALIA

Max was dead. Galen had lost his father, but I couldn't help feeling as though I'd lost one as well. After my father was murdered, Max had filled the gap, stepping into a role that neither of us intended for him to fill.

And yet he had.

He'd been an emotional support since I first joined the Long Claw pack, offering me advice and caring. I couldn't help feeling that he was looking out for me during the ceremony. Maybe he sensed something was wrong through the pack bond and held on long enough to help me.

It was unbearable to consider that his death might be the reason I was still alive.

I knew he'd been secretly rooting for us to be a couple and I'd been looking forward to sharing a PG-rated version of how Galen and I had taken things to the next level.

But now I'd never get to tell him.

He'd never see Galen married or have children of his own. He'd never watch Galen become the man and the true Alpha we all knew he could be.

It wasn't supposed to happen. It shouldn't have happened. Wolves don't get sick. Not like that. We don't die from an unnamed infection. We healed ourselves.

But in the end, all our strength, all the magic that bound our forms together, didn't matter.

Max died anyway.

I packed our bags, because Galen was clearly in shock, and made the arrangements for the trip home.

Under the circumstances, the valet service made an exception to their no-vehicles beyond the main gate policy and brought our trucks to the cabin.

Galen was in no condition to drive.

I took the keys and loaded the suitcases into the bed of the truck and headed back inside to collect Galen.

A knock sounded at the door.

"I'll send whoever it is away. You don't have to talk to anyone right now. It's okay." I bent down and kissed his cheek, then headed over to answer the door.

Valerie and Victor stood on the front porch, each with a bundle of wildflowers.

I thought they'd come to offer their condolences, which they did, but there was another reason for their visit.

"We need to speak with you." Victor motioned for me to join them outside for a private conversation.

"I appreciate you stopping by, but whatever it is, it's going to have to wait." I glanced over my shoulder at where Galen sat silent. "It's not a good time."

"There won't ever be a good time, Talia." Valerie's sad smile matched the look in her eyes. "You've been searching for one for days and haven't found one."

"We know about your eyes." Victor blurted it out, like ripping off a bandage.

"It's why you wouldn't shift with the others." Valerie

explained how they came to that conclusion. "Some wolves from our pack carry a unique trait."

"Red eyes are a unique trait?" I asked, mortified that they knew and seemed to think it was a good thing and not something to be ashamed of.

"It can lie dormant in some wolves." Valerie reached for my hand, but I jerked back before she could touch me.

"Twenty-five years dormant? You're not making any sense. Either of you."

"We were born into a pack of demon wolves, and we think you were, too. We don't share the red eyed trait. It's reserved for royalty." Victor wrung his hands together. "You have red eyes. It's the only explanation. It has to be you."

Demon wolves? Royalty? "No, there has to be another reason. I just have to figure out what it is." It turned to go back inside. "You're both crazy. Certifiable, you know that? Demon wolves and royalty. What is a demon wolf anyway? I've never heard such a thing in all my life."

"Talia, wait. We're not crazy. You said it yourself. It was a weird coincidence that we were all here at this summit together." Valerie was sprite for an old woman and jumped in front of the door, blocking me from going inside. "But you don't believe in coincidences, do you?"

"No," I muttered, more to myself than either of them. "I don't."

Valerie pleaded for me to listen to them. Not to walk away until I heard what she had to say.

"Red eyes are a royal trait, passed down from generation to generation. There has only been one princess born to our pack in the last century. She was stolen the day she was born, and we haven't stopped searching for her. It's been twenty-five years."

"Twenty-five years?" I repeated in disbelief.

Red eyes? Demon wolves. Royal blood. The princess was the

same age as me? So many similarities. But they were all just coin-cidences.

Except, I didn't believe in coincidences.

~

THE END... continued in Wolf of Bones.
Pre-order: https://books2read.com/wolfofbones